I0747795

PECK FINCH and the EIGHT OF SWORDS

A Peck Finch Novel

Jerome Mark Antil

Copyright © Jerome Mark Antil 2022

ISBN: 978-1-7378572-8-0
(Paperback Edition)

Library of Congress Control Number: 2022915396

All characters appearing in this work are fictitious. Any resemblance to real persons, living or dead, is purely coincidental.

Heartfelt Thanks To:

My Pamela; Marty Bays; Rick Clancy

No part of this publication may be reproduced, stored in a retrieval system, or transmitted in any form or by any means electronic, mechanical, photocopying, recording, or otherwise, without the written permission of the author or publisher.

1.

IT WAS THE NIGHT THE ICE CAME. The hot tin roof of the eighteenth-century, shotgun-turned jazz bar—in an alley off Frenchman Street—was being peppered like a drummer's snare. Whenever hail knocked on the Big Easy, jazz would mute. The band sat it out, sipping scotch.

Peck stood to leave.

"Clean another night, Peck," Lily Cup said. "It must be crazy cold out there, with everything iced up."

Peck, Cajun French, in his mid-twenties, was a celebrated "eye of an eagle" tracker with instincts he learned surviving reptile-infested swamps and bayous of Acadiana barefoot since he was five. He'd earn his keep doing private investigative work for Lily Cup's criminal law practice and for police lieutenant Larry Gaines. On Sunday nights he'd clean Sasha's real estate offices on Napoleon and Lily Cup's law office on Carrolton, rain or shine. And it was Sunday night. He took his work and his word seriously.

Peck played with his key FOB, offered a polite wave, turned and went to the bar.

"Charlie, can I ax could I pay tomorrow, frien'?"

Charlie had a Master's degree in political science from Mississippi State—but he was a good bartender and a good friend, and he would play into Peck's natural Cajun *patois* as a pal.

"Pay for what, bébé—?"

"—for everybody at our table? With the racket, ain't been no dancing. Thought I'd pick up my frien's tab but I'm—how you say—a little short."

"Git' outta' heya—go earn you some green, bébé," Charlie replied. "I know where you at."

"Thanks, frien'."

Then, like a big yawn can sometime make a *pop* in your ear, the racket on the tin roof stopped. The tenor sax player began mouthing his reed like a popsicle stick—moistening it for a jazz riff that would bring the evening alive again.

Peck left the Blue Note.

In the time it would have taken him to walk the alley from Charlie's Blue Note to Frenchman Street the explosion shook the old house and the ground around it. The boom's concussion cracked the mirror behind the bar and a wall hanging neon beer sign crashed to the floor.

"What the fu—?" Gabe shouted.

"That was on Frenchman Street," Larry said.

He stood, felt a pocket for his badge.

"Peck's pickup!" Lily Cup screamed. "His pickup blew up when he started it. They've killed Peck."

Everyone froze in their seats, already thinking how to eulogize their Cajun French friend.

When it came to personal tragedy New Orleans was like no other place.

In the city of *gris-gris,* physical survival was more hope than promise. The front porch to Gulf winds storming Acadiana like Barbary coast pirates. Politicians destroying nature's ecosystem in Southern Louisiana, permitting the lumbering and chipping of thousand-year-old giant cypress trees into mulch, turning swamps lifeless. That, and a history of Mississippi River dams flooding without warning, burying Acadians alive—their homes, their churches drowned in suffocating silt and discharging lives and dreams, bleeding them into the Gulf.

Denial was the best defense, so most chose *celebration* for distraction—whether it be costumed parades up St. Charles Avenue, or funeral dirges with a Dixieland trombone, a tuba and a drummer man. They'd buy guns to fend off the vultures whose scavenging followed storms like rats in a city dump.

Lily Cup stood to go look.

"I told him they'd bomb his pickup," Lily Cup said.

"Who?" Gabe asked.

"The sex traffickers," Lily Cup said.

"Sit down," Larry said. "It's not Peck's pickup."

"Like you'd know from in here," Lily Cup said.

"I know from in here because he started it from in here—before he left the table."

"He did?"

"He stood right here—started it after you mentioned the ice."

"You sure?"

"I watched him start it. It would have exploded then."

Lily Cup sat down, took a gulp of her rye.

"Where's Sasha?" Larry asked.

"She went to pee," Lily Cup said.

"Folks, stay calm. Stay in here," Larry said.

"My brother," Gabe said.

Larry was rushing to the door when the second explosion rattled the jazz bar's window shutters. This time Charlie jumped over the bar and met him at the door.

"Doesn't sound good, eh?" Charlie asked.

Larry opened the door to a rolling thermal brightness of billowing flames illuminating Frenchman Street.

He spoke in a low voice.

"That's a petroleum fire. Charlie, you wait here."

He pulled his revolver and cautiously made his way through the ice-crusted alley to Frenchman Street. He looked about—stopped short, holstered his gun and ran back to Charlie in the doorway.

"It's Peck."

"Ah nah—God damn!" Charlie said.

Larry pressed his mic button.

"Headquarters, this is unit nine-eight-four—I'm at one-two-three Frenchman Street."

"Sasha's out there too," Charlie said.

"Are you serious, Charlie?"

"Copy nine-eight-four," a voice barked.

"I need units to respond—a vehicle just exploded."

"Copy nine-eight-four."

"Charlie, are you positive Sasha—?" Larry started.

"Peck left his phone on the bar—she ran it out."

"Anyone asks what's up—you don't know, Charlie."

"How about Lily Cup—how about ol' Gabe?"

"Especially not them, Charlie. No time to explain."

"You got my word, bébé. Be careful out there."

"You have a back door?"

"Behind the kitchen."

"If anybody insists on leaving—use it."

"If they do, they're not welcome back," Charlie said.

Larry hurried to Frenchman Street, watching flames and wary of more explosions.

"Checking for injuries," he said into his mic. "Send EMS—fire—have units cut traffic into this area."

"Copy, Lieutenant," a voice said.

"If Officer Downs is on duty, dispatch him."

"Copy, Lieutenant, this is Downs—I'm on my way."

Larry blessed himself with the sign of the cross. He whispered, "Peck and Michelle, it will never be the same without you two."

He stepped off the curb.

"I hate my work."

Peck had been accepted into Tulane's night school. He read a book a week—preferred John Steinbeck to Tolstoy—and was enjoying Hemingway. Their table at Charlie's Blue Note on dance nights would be friends who'd come to dance jazz—the retired career army captain, a Creole named Gabe, the real estate magnate and Acadian French Michelle Lisette (who always went by "Sasha" at Charlie's Blue Note) Sasha's best friend (since they were six), Lily Cup, the cigar-smoking Harvard Law grad and criminal attorney, and Lily Cup's brown sugar and high school basketball flame and now grown-up police lieutenant, Larry. Gabe and Lieutenant Larry were like black bookends to an unlikely assortment of characters at any table in Southern Louisiana.

Peck had captured hearts.

2.

LARRY'S FLASHLIGHT GUIDED HIM through the ice. He stepped off the curb and walked toward the flaming pickup as if looking for Peck's and Sasha's bodies. A shower of hail pellets fell like beads thrown from a float at Mardi Gras from their nest on the oak branches above. He brushed them off.

"Larry!"

A wind gust muffled the sounds.

"Over here!"

Larry looked around, full circle.

"Larry?"

"Peck?"

"Larry!"

"Peck, is that you?"

Larry followed the voice and saw a woman's bloody leg with a shoeless foot laying on the sidewalk. He elbow-pushed his way into and through a thick growth of bushes. He found Peck down, lying on top of Sasha, both covered in ice and buried in needle-sharp, prickly holly bush twigs. He leaned over.

"Peck, you're alive."

Peck lifted his head.

"Thank God," Larry said.

Peck's hair was singed and there was blood on his forehead from holly bush branch cuts.

"Talk to me. Either of you hurt?"

"I'm okay," Peck said. "I don't know about—"

"Don't move until we have you checked out for broken bones," Larry said.

"I'm all right," Sasha moaned, her cheek resting on the icy ground. Her eyes opened.

"I think I broke my wrist," she whimpered.

"How about your leg, Sasha?"

Sasha touched a thigh with her hand.

"I can't feel this leg."

"The calf looks pretty bloody. Don't move it."

Peck raised his arm for help.

Larry carefully pulled him to his feet.

"Careful of Sasha, son," Larry said.

Peck stepped back.

"Sasha, let me check your wrist," Larry said.

She held it up.

"What happened?" Sasha asked.

"Still checking," Larry said.

"Was that a bomb?" Sasha asked.

"Think maybe."

"Where?"

"Peck's pickup."

"Why would someone put a bomb in Peck's pickup?"

Larry didn't answer.

"Did somebody try to kill Peck?" Sasha asked.

"Your face is badly scratched up, Sasha. Did you hit your head?"

"No."

"You sure? I have EMS coming."

"I remember hitting the bushes and landing on my hand. I'm positive."

Larry handed his flashlight to Peck. He examined Sasha's wrist as sirens approached. Three patrol cars drove up, one was Officer Downs. Downs parked at the alley to Charlie's Blue Note and waited for Larry's signal.

"Your wrist isn't broken—you landed hard—maybe a sprain—it'll hurt a spell."

"You sure?"

"I'm sure. Don't put pressure on that leg until we have it looked at," Larry said.

He and Peck helped her to her feet.

"Who would want to—? Sasha started.

Larry interrupted in a whisper.

"Listen up—both of you."

"Okay," Peck said.

"I won't lie. This has all the signs of a hit—"

"*Aye yi-yi*," Peck said.

"—until we can check it out, forensics, witnesses. If it was a hit and they know you're alive, they won't give up."

"Jesus, Mary, and Joseph!" Sasha said.

"Peck—just nod your head—you got a place you can hide?"

Peck nodded.

"Sasha, don't move your lips—whisper. Where's your car?" Larry asked.

"The Be—" Sasha started to answer, before Larry covered her mouth with his fingers, muffling her.

"Your car…no details," Larry whispered.

"Garage on Decatur," Sasha whispered.

"How's the leg?"

"I can feel it a little. It's asleep from Peck landing on me."

"I need you two to hide until I get answers. Peck, take Sasha with you to hide out—I'll get you to her car."

Larry flagged Officer Downs over.

"Why me?" Sasha asked. "Why do I have to hide?"

"Honey, if this was a hit and they know he's alive— they won't think twice—grabbing you to trade for Peck."

"Mother of God," Sasha said.

Using Larry's flashlight Peck knelt on the sidewalk, examining Sasha's leg. He pulled glass from it.

"This needs to be covered," Peck said.

Officer Downs reached his arm over the seatback and held a box of bandages for Peck.

Larry opened the back door of the patrol car. Peck helped Sasha in.

"Have that leg and her face looked at when you get where you're going, son," Larry said.

"Won't they follow us?" Sasha whispered. "They're probably watching now."

"They're gone—but their game is afoot," Larry said.

"That's comforting, Sherlock," Sasha quipped.

Peck leaned over Sasha's lap and whispered. "Tell Gabe we're okay, Larry?"

Larry bent on a knee and whispered back. "Crime scene rule—you never know who's listening or recording a video. Charlie's is packed. For your safety I'll tell them when the time is right."

"He's an ol' man, Larry—his heart can't—"

"Son, Gabe's a brother—a fellow vet—I'll give him the wink."

"The wink?"

"He'll know you're okay and he'll know not to talk."

"Understand, frien', thanks," Peck said. "Can you find my book, Larry?"

"Book, son? What book?"

"I had me a John Grisham, Lily Cup gave me. It's got to be somewhere."

"So that's what nearly broke my wrist—your book?" Sasha asked.

Larry shook his head.

"Officer Downs, take them where the lady says."

"Yes, Lieutenant," Officer Downs said.

"And tail 'em until you're sure no one's following."

"Yes, Lieutenant."

Larry leaned down and spoke into the window of the patrol car.

"Don't use phones. You get a call, especially if you know who's calling—don't answer unless it's me calling. In fact, turn 'em off until morning."

"Can I call Lily Cup?" Sasha asked.

"Especially not Lily Cup. If they're tracking phones, that'll signal them and they'll know Peck's alive. Worse, they'll know where you both are."

A firefighter walked up to Larry and handed him a Louboutin shoe and broken heel. Larry held them for Sasha and pushed the door closed.

The patrol car sped away, down Frenchman Street.

3.

NO ONE AT THE TABLE was aware that Sasha had gone outside. Gabe, her dance partner, knew two things—he knew the band had started a riff worth dancing, and she wasn't there. And Sasha never missed a dance. He had anxious in his eyes, but he was a thirty-year veteran, and the military in him required patience and silence, with eyes peeled. Lily Cup was edgy with Larry still outside. She lit a cigar and lifted her rye for a sip.

Peck meant a lot to her. They had a past, and now they were close friends and confidants. Peck raised himself from being a nine-year-old runaway—illiterate and abused in snake-infested swamps to that of being accepted in Tulane's night school, reading a book a week. He'd supported himself since he was nine by casting nets, fishing with trot lines—bartering his catches for food—and by mowing the lawn at a hospice in Carencro, where he first met Gabe. He used his skill for sharpening saw blades in trade for a sleeping cot in a boat builder's shed and the roof over his head.

As they did frequently, this unlikely group of friends gathered at Charlie's Blue Note to dance and enjoy the best live jazz and red beans and rice in New Orleans. Sasha in finest haute in strapless gowns and designer shoes loved to dance with jazz man Gabe—retired Army captain, decorated in Korea and Viet Nam—the best dancer she's ever been with on the floor. Before Peck went outside, he was at the table reading a book Lily Cup had slid across the table to him—John Grisham's *The Rainmaker*.

As Officer Downs's patrol car turned off Frenchman Street with Sasha and Peck, Larry's two-way squawked.

"We've got a body, Lieutenant!"

"Copy," Larry responded.

He pressed a button.

"This is nine-eight-four."

"Copy, nine-eight-four—come back."

"We need the coroner—on Frenchman Street."

"Copy that, Lieutenant. We'll send O'Sullivan."

Firefighters who had cordoned off the charred pickup with crime scene tape let Larry through as forensics had taken whatever evidence they had found. Larry stepped around the truck's frame and saw a body covered with foam. It was lying on its back, its head on the curb. Its face was burned to the bone.

"This never gets easy," Larry said.

"Never, sir."

"Is that a tuxedo?"

"Think so, Lieutenant. Forensics found a bow tie on the sidewalk. His shoes were black patent leather—they took them too, sir."

Larry pointed at the pickup's door.

"Was the door like this when you got here, or did forensics open it?"

"Not sure, sir."

"It's open, Officer—this door has been opened."

4.

OFFICER DOWNS DROVE UP and stepped out to report to Larry. He leaned in for privacy.

"Followed 'em past Metairie, Lieutenant. No tail."

"Good job, Downs. I'm going into Charlie's—sure the natives are getting restless. When they bag the body and not until it's driven away—two-way me a code *eighty-six*—got it, Downs?"

"Got it, Lieutenant."

"Good man."

"What is code *eighty-six*, Lieutenant?"

"It's my code—means unlock the door. I made it up when I was a kid playing cops and robbers. It'll release the hounds inside Charlie's. This crowd lives Big Easy blues like it's Purgatory, and this is all in a night's entertainment. They'll hang here like moss on cypress."

"Gotcha, sir."

"Answer no questions, Downs—tell our crew, no talking—to people, to media."

"Yes sir."

"Tell them it's an order."

"I'll get the word out, Lieutenant."

As Larry stepped in the alley to Charlie's Blue Note, Peck and Sasha were on I-10 passing Lake Ponchartrain. No sign of hail, but the full moon reflected off intimidating whitecaps of the haunted lake. Sasha's head leaned back on the headrest. She appeared to be entranced, face scratched like a grade school tomboy being hypnotized by the moon and the *gris-gris* of a new life chapter the night served up and to New Orleans, making it personal. Neither had spoken a word since leaving the scene on Frenchman Street. Best guess, both were frozen in the reality that it was attempted murder. Sasha from nearly being killed—Peck from knowing he's prey for the first time since he was an abused child chained under gator man's porch. He's not the hunter tonight. He's the prey—the target.

"J'ai besoin que tu me fasses un appel, cher," Peck said. ("I need you to make me a call, cher.")

"Larry a dit pas d'appels, Peck," Sasha said. ("Larry said no calls, Peck.")

"I need to call Bait Man Alex—tell him we coming."

Peck turned his phone on and handed it to her to look up Bait Man Alex's number. Four calls from Lily Cup appeared on the screen. She ignored their flashes, opened the contact page and found Bait Man Alex. She pressed the number into her phone, turned Peck's phone off and handed it and her phone to Peck.

"This is late for a call," Bait Man Alex said.

"It's me, frien'—how you all are?"

"This you, Peck?"

"Ah *oui*."

"Sounds like trouble, you calling late like this. Is it something about your momma?"

"Nah-nah—but we on our way and it's purdy late and I need to let Mamma know we coming and not be scared when she sees Sasha's Bentley drive up to the houseboat."

"How long are you coming for, Peck? Should I toss the traps? I got plenty of chicken necks bagged up."

"Did I wake you, frien?"

"I was reading—now I'm hosing bait coolers—I was up."

"If you want to toss the traps, we pass a good time in the morning. I got Sasha with me."

"Is everything okay, Peck?"

"I'll explain when I get there. You got something for skin cuts?"

"Already don't like the sounds of things, my friend. I'll bring some bandages and medicine."

"Did it hail where you at, frien'?"

"Not here, but I see you got dumped on pretty good. The wife and I watched it on the news. When will you be driving in?"

"Two—maybe one hour. See you soon."

Peck ended the call and handed the phone to Sasha.

"Look at my dress," Sasha said. "Ripped, blood on it—ten-thousand-dollar Givenchy. My favorite jazz dancing dress. Look at the shoe—Louboutin … everything's ruined."

"Tu veux la bonne nouvelle, cher?" ("You want the good news, cher?")

Sasha laughed. *"Tu es tellement drôle."* ("You are so funny.")

"Moi?" ("Me?")

"No wonder Acadian women want to climb on you."

"Nah-nah, cher. Peck's a good boy."

"It's such a turn on."

"What is, how you say—a turn on?"

"Your confidence."

Sasha tossed the shoe and heel into the back seat.

"So, give it. Peck. I could use some good news."

"We're alive, cher, that's for one …"

"Tellement vrai," ("So true.") "Look at my face, Peck—the cuts and scratches."

"Can't see your face, cher, but I see your *girls* with that purdy moon shining on them through the window. Oh my—that's good for lookin'—ain't looking at scratches."

Sasha glanced down at her cleavage—*her girls*—put a flat hand over them, feigning modesty as might a school girl at a first prom. She smirked and leaned her head back, feeling a calming effect being with Peck, the man who had saved her life. She unbuckled and reached for her gym bag on the back floor. With it in hand she turned and sat forward in the seat.

"Zip?"

With eyes on the road, Peck reached back and unzipped her Givenchy. Sasha sat up and while contorting her torso, pulled it off and down to the floor, pushing out of it with her toes. She reached behind her waist, unfastened her garter belt and pulled it and her stockings down and off. Her left thigh had an eight-inch dark purple bruise. She stared at it in silence. She touched it as if to see if it hurt. She reached down and touched the bandages on her calf.

"These cuts are going to scar," Sasha muttered.

"They're memories, cher, when you old and gray."

"If tonight is any indication of what it's going to be like—hanging with you—I'll be gray soon."

"Night's not over, cher."

Sasha howled.

She unhooked her black strapless bra, letting her firm breasts push it off and onto her lap. She pulled her gym tights up to her waist and a sweatshirt over her head. Before buckling the seatbelt, she leaned over the console and gave Peck a kiss on the cheek.

"Thanks for being you, Peck."

Peck smiled.

"Thanks for saving my life."

"Ever think, cher—by you being with me, bringing me my phone like you did—you saved Peck's life?"

Sasha's eyes misted. She sat back.

"Take you some rest, bébé. We be at Mamma's soon. We'll pass a good time—maybe settle down—boil some crabs, suck some tails. Amite River, the Canal and Mamma's houseboat just a snooze away, cher. Close them purdy eyes."

5.

PECK PULLED THE BENTLEY onto the river bank near the willow tree Mamma's houseboat was tied to. Bait Man Alex was tossing the last of twenty crab traps, ten on either side. Peck's Mamma was awake and on deck in pajamas, smiling and waiting.

Peck stepped out.

"I don't know to be happy or nervous," Mamma said. "Sasha, come in out of the chill—I have the wood stove going."

"Hi Mamma," Sasha said, waving from the Bentley.

Peck hugged Bait Man Alex hello, and not trusting the dew-covered ladder, he picked Sasha up from the car and lifted her onto the houseboat.

"Careful of her leg, Mamma."

"Your face, Sasha—are you all right, dear?"

"I'm okay, Mamma."

Sasha and Mamma stepped inside for warmth.

It was a modest houseboat, gifted to Mamma by Dr. Pontelbon when Peck was born. Dr. Pontelbon cared for Mémé, Mamma's mother at the Psychiatrique Hospital. Peck was the result of Mamma getting raped by an orderly when she was in her early twenties visiting Mémé. When Peck was eight, Mamma didn't know Peck had run away—abused by a man she thought was a family friend. The gator man would chain young Peck under a porch and tape his mouth to keep him from screaming while being pulled behind a boat in dark, snake-infested bayou swamps as bait to attract alligators. Mamma and Dr. Pontelbon believed an alligator got him when he was nine while playing. She learned gardening and supports herself bicycling to homes and businesses caring for their flora. She visits Mémé twice a week and reads to her. The doc passed away five years ago, but he shared the story of Peck's family history through a letter he wanted to be read to Peck if he was ever found alive. He left the letter of the legend with his best friend, the banker, Mr. Hebert. Peck still visits Mr. Hebert on occasion to say hello and to listen to the stories.

"The place is pretty small, Sasha—you can have my bed."

"Mamma, I would never put you out," Sasha said. "We'll figure something—don't worry, we'll manage."

Sasha noticed three pairs of men's boxer briefs on a side table.

"Are those Peck's?" she asked.

"They are—he left them, I washed them."

Sasha picked one up.

"Think he'll mind?" Sasha asked.

Mamma grinned.

Sasha pulled her tights to the floor, stepped out, picked them up and folded them. Mamma gasped at seeing the bruise on Sasha's thigh, but she would wait for the story. Her Peck was always clear and honest about telling her the truth. Sasha stepped in a pair of Peck's boxer briefs and pulled them up.

"That's better," she said. "It's toasty warm in here."

Sasha and Mamma sat at the table and waited for the men. The houseboat rocked gently as Peck climbed aboard. He came through the door alone.

"Is Alex coming in?" Mamma asked.

"Bait Man Alex, he gone, Mamma. He tossed the traps—good frien'. He'll be here in the morning. We'll have a boil and suck some tails."

"Do you have any wine?" Sasha asked.

Mamma took a corked bottle of red from the cabinet and handed it and a glass to Sasha.

"This should still be good," Mamma said. "I use it on salads."

Mamma sat and with a cotton ball she touched the scratches on Sasha's face with an antiseptic.

"Why have you come, Boudreaux? It's not First Friday. Why so late?"

She pointed at the bruise on Sasha's leg.

"Something's wrong, son—what's wrong?"

Peck paused, took a deep inhale of a nostalgic warmth and smells of burning firewood. He pulled a cover torn paperback copy of a book from his back pocket. It was Hemingway's *The Old Man and the Sea*. Peck held it up and sat down.

"This is a short book—not much to it, Mamma—but it's an important book. The lady at the used book store told me Mr. Hemingway was given an important prize—how you say, Nobel Prize—for writing it."

"I know the book, Boudreaux. Haven't read it, but I know of it."

"You know why it's an important book, Mamma?"

"I don't, son."

"Because it tells the truth from its first word. It don't beat around—how you say—no bush, Mamma. It comes out and tells straight off. ... listen to this:"

Peck opened the book and began reading.

"He was an old man who fished alone in a skiff in the Gulf Stream and he had gone eighty-four days without taking a fish. But after forty days without a fish the boy's parents had told him that the old man was now definitely and finally 'salao' which is the worst form of unlucky ...

"It goes on like that, Mamma, but see how Mr. Hemingway just come right out and tell it like it is? Can you see that, Mamma?"

"Boudreaux, what are you trying to tell me?"

"Mamma, somebody put a bomb in my pickup and it blowed up. They tried to kill me, and Lieutenant Gaines told us to go hide, and that's why we come here."

"This happened tonight?"

"Yes, Mamma."

"Were you near the pickup?"

"We were across the street."

Mamma blessed herself with a sign of the cross.

"We fell in bushes when it happened. Sasha cut her leg, see her face, Mamma? Lieutenant told us to go hide—that's why we come here so late."

Mamma held Sasha's hand.

"Are you all right, dear?" Mamma asked.

"I'm shaking like a leaf, Mamma," Sasha said. "Peck's been a good shoulder to lean on. It'll take time, but I'll be okay in time."

"Boudreaux, no more talk of this. Sasha needs you tonight. Clear your heads. We'll talk in the morning. You both take my bed. I'll sleep here on the pull-out. It's upholstered and comfortable."

"Mamma, you don't—" Sasha started.

"Not another word," Mamma said.

She handed Sasha a lighted candle to take into the bedroom. Peck guided her.

"Pull the curtain open, cher. They's a full moon," Peck said.

Peck and Sasha sank into the feather mattress clutching each other while being cradled by a gentle rocking of the warm, friendly houseboat tied to the shore. They fell asleep sharing a pillow.

6.

IT WAS 3:00 a.m. and lights were on in Gabe's shotgun. Larry pulled into the driveway. The path to the side door was icy, but as he made it up the steps the door opened with Lily Cup holding a pot of chicory.

"You go to hell," Lily Cup barked.

"That's a fine howdy—how did I deserve that?"

"It was Peck's pickup, wasn't it?"

"It was."

"In Charlie's, you told us it wasn't his pickup."

"At the time, I didn't think it was."

"Who's dead, Larry—did Peck get hurt? Sasha, is she okay?"

"Who told you somebody's dead?"

"Larry!" Lily Cup barked.

"Peck and Sasha are okay," Larry said.

With a sigh, Lily Cup straightened her posture as if it were the first time since the explosions. She lifted a coffee mug and held it out for Larry.

"How'd you know about—? Larry started.

"Need a drink, sailor?"

Larry closed the door behind him, took the coffee and leaned down for a kiss.

"Where are they?" Lily Cup asked.

"How'd you know about a victim?" Larry asked.

"I called Chris—the coroner—he said the dead guy was wearing a tuxedo—couldn't be Peck."

"When did you sneak out of Charlie's?"

"We went out the back door—after the second explosion. Gabe saw you pulling your gun. We figured Peck blew up with his pickup. I've been warning him about that— car bombs. Charlie wouldn't let us come out to Frenchman Street and wouldn't tell us anything until I threatened to kick his ass. He told us Sasha was out there too—and I fainted. We figured it was over."

"What a night," Larry said.

"Charlie was pissed we left—but he understood."

"He'll get over it. You're a favorite of his."

"You done for the night?" Lily Cup asked.

They stepped into the living room. Gabe was leaning back on his recliner.

"My brother," Gabe said. "Take a load off—rest your bones."

Lily Cup squatted on the rug in front of Larry as if she were a child waiting for a bedtime story.

"Millie coming here after graduation?" Larry asked.

"Peck and Millie are taking a break," Lily Cup said.

"Oh? Since when?" Larry asked.

"She doesn't know it yet. I'll tell you later," Lily Cup said.

"Should I step out of the room?" Gabe asked.

"Stay, Gabe," Lily Cup said. "Larry, later?"

Larry nodded.

"Those explosions scared us, Larry. We were sure Peck and Sasha were dead."

"I was too," Larry said.

No one spoke, as if taking it in again—steeped in thought. The night was pivotal in their lives. Knowing bombs dedicated at taking the life of one of their own seemed to change everything.

"To get the record straight, Larry. It was only Peck's pickup that blew up, right?" Lily Cup asked.

"It was."

"Why were there two explosions?"

"Forensics is trying to figure that out."

"You promise they're both okay."

"I do. We'll know more in the morning."

"You're keeping something from me, Larry. What're you not telling me?"

"Been at it hours, woman—can we wait until morning to see what's shakin'?"

"That's bullshit, Larry. You keep us in the dark and we're supposed to tuck in bed and not think about it? Not fair," Lily Cup said.

"Forensics and Chris are working all night on it—we're trying to keep names out of the press," Larry said.

"Who's really dead?" Lily Cup asked. "Don't lie to me, Larry. Did Chris lie to me? Are Peck and Sasha dead?"

"Sasha had some glass in her leg. She sprained a wrist. Scratched up her face. They were thirty feet from the truck when it exploded. Peck saved her. Both are fine, I promise."

"I believe you."

"Could of been a hit meant for Peck."

"Ya' think?" Lily Cup asked sarcastically.

"Maybe for his busting up the trafficker ring—"

"Of course," Lily Cup said.

"But Peck does investigative work for us, Lily Cup. He investigates for your criminal trials and he does private investigative work for me, a cop. This bomb could have been targeting any one of us."

"Who's dead, Larry?" Lily Cup asked. "Who's the guy in the tuxedo?"

"Chris told you that much?"

"I didn't believe him that it wasn't Peck until he told me the guy was wearing a tuxedo. He only told me that when I thought Peck was dead and he was covering it up—he wasn't ratting you out—he was trying to convince me it wasn't Peck."

"We should have answers in the morning."

"Hold on," Lily Cup said.

She pressed Millie's contact number on her phone.

"Hello?"

"Millie, where are you, honey? Waco or at home in North Carolina?"

"I got home last night. Why are you calling so early? It's 3:20. What's wrong?"

"Honey, I've got some news—it's about Peck."

"He hasn't been answering my calls. Is he okay?"

"I didn't want you hearing rumors without knowing the truth."

"Oh no."

"He's okay, Millie—honest—but last night someone put a bomb in his pickup and it exploded."

Millie screamed.

"No!"

"Thank God he wasn't in it."

"My God—is Peck okay?"

"He's fine—the police have him hiding somewhere for his own protection—just don't worry."

"*Merciful Jesus*. He must be so scared."

"Peck is strong, Millie—you know better than most."

"Thank you for calling. I'll pray for him."

"Good night, sweetie."

The call ended.

"That was thoughtful, little sister," Gabe said.

"Can I take you home, woman?" Larry asked. "I've got a long drive to Covington."

"Stay at my place, Larry. I'll follow you. I'm not letting you drive the causeway—it's iced up," Lily Cup said.

"I need a tub and sleep," Larry said.

"Stay with me," Lily Cup said. "I'm sorry about the sass. It's just that—"

"Your friends Sasha and Peck too —I understand," Larry said. "I can imagine the torture you went through."

"You have brandy, little sister?" Gabe asked.

Lily Cup stood up.

"I have some," she said.

"Hear me out," Gabe said.

Lily Cup stood with Larry. They held hands.

"Whatever happens, folks. Look at what we are, my brother—little sister—look at what we had at that table tonight—that's our family," Gabe said. "Different colors, different ethnicity, religions—we're family. It took jazz and a dance floor to bring us together, but we're family now. Sometimes brothers or sisters go to their room—need space. Some air—a need to breathe. But in the end, a family never forgets why we are—who our brothers and sisters are—and it's our values that make everything good and right, and it's those values that bring us back together. Our togetherness is our strength."

"Amen, my brother," Larry said.

"I feel like I'm at a black gospel meeting," Lily Cup said. "But I agree."

"Sleep warm, you two—salt 'n pepper," Gabe said.

Lily Cup took Larry by the hand.

"I have every intention of sleeping warm," Lily Cup mused. "Come on, Pepper."

"Silver Whistle Café for breakfast, brother?" Larry asked. "It'll be my treat. Just you and me, Gabe."

"Only have to honk once, my brother. I'll be out," Gabe said.

Gabe walked them to the kitchen door, closed and bolted it behind them and turned the lights off.

7.

BEAMS OF A MORNING SUN SPRINKLED through blinds like spotlights on the antique makeup table, once belonging to Lily Cup's mother. It was Lily Cup's now and stacked with law books. Larry was alone in her bed. His phone buzzed. He reached for it.

"Talk to me."

"Rick Clancy—Forensics, Lieutenant."

"Whatcha got, Clancy?"

"Coroner O'Sullivan wants you to call him later, but asked me to let you know we have an all clear on the bomb, Lieutenant. It wasn't a hit. Should be safe for the targets to resume life. Where do you want me to fax my notes?"

"Sounds like a Shakespearian comedy, Forensics—a bomb goes off in a man's vehicle and it wasn't a hit—and the targets can resume life? Give me a break!"

"Lieutenant—Coroner O'Sullivan told me you'd say something like that, but he insisted I tell you the targets are safe to come out of hiding, and he'll explain everything when you come to his lab. He'd like you there at 2:00 p.m. if you can make it. He asked that you call first."

"I'll need more than that, Rick. No offense, but why didn't Chris call me?"

"He's doing autopsy—said to tell you his hands were full this morning."

"Fax me what you've got to Lily Cup Tarleton's fax—you have the number?"

"I'm sure we do. If not, I'll call you back."

"Tell Chris I'll be there."

Larry clicked his phone off and tossed it on the bed just as Lily Cup came in the room in yellow panties with LSU stenciled in black on the rear, and a Harvard Law T-shirt. She was carrying two mugs of cinnamon chicory coffee.

"Morning handsome," Lily Cup mused. "I was going to give you a friendly goodnight about four but you were fast asleep when your head hit the pillow. You never even pulled the blanket up."

"Lily Cup," Larry said. "Without any varnish, tell me what happened between Peck and Millie."

"Nothing's happened, but it's about to."

"Keep it simple—I don't want a soap."

"Simple answer? When they fell in love, he was a good guy. He's still a good guy, but now he's a murderer and only you and me and a priest know. He's murdered two bad guys. Does he lie to her by omission and stay, living with the lie, or does he tell her and hope she stays with him?"

"What a mess," Larry said.

"You asked for no varnish. Drink your coffee."

"Just got an all clear," Larry said.

"All clear—as in—?"

"It's safe—they can come home."

Lily Cup took Larry's phone and called Sasha's iPhone.

With a musky wakeup mumble, Sasha answered:

"Larry?"

"It's me, sweet pea," Lily Cup said.

"What time is it?"

"It's safe for you guys to come home."

"It is?"

"Go back to sleep."

Larry took the phone from Lily Cup.

"Sasha, tell Peck I need him here at 1:30."

"Okay," Sasha whispered.

They ended the call.

"Who's that, bébé," Peck whispered.

"Go back to sleep."

"What time is it?"

Sasha lifted a bruised thigh over Peck's legs, nudged a morning William, rested a bent knee on his abs.

"Shh—go back to sleep," she whispered.
She kissed his ear.

Larry picked Gabe up for a drive to breakfast at the Silver Whistle Café in the Ponchartrain Hotel on St. Charles Avenue. They found a table and sat.

"My brother," Gabe said. "We need wisdom this morning—let's start with eggs, light scrambled for me and the biggest breakfast roll you've got—saucer of gravy, bottle of Louisiana hot sauce to stoke the fire."

The server was writing on a pad.

"We don't do wisdom here, sir, at least not before ten," the server quipped, "but anything else we can do. Butter and cream in your eggs?"

"Perfect—and you said you don't do wisdom," Gabe said.

"Boudin? Grits?" the server asked.

Gabe raised his palms as in a surrendering *"How can I resist?"*

"Same," Larry said. He held his menu up for her to take.

"Come up with anything?" Gabe asked.

"Forensics have done a job. I think they're tired of me finding clues they leave behind. Except for one thing, I found they're pretty spot-on this time."

"Who wants Peck dead?" Gabe asked.

"That's just it, brother—nobody wants him dead. Not this time, anyway."

Gabe sipped coffee, not taking his eyes off Larry.

"No way Forensics could come up with that, could they?" Gabe asked.

"The bomb was attached months ago, Gabe."

"The sex traffickers," Gabe mumbled.

Larry nodded.

"The device was triggered to go off months ago. It was meant to be a hit—but it never went off—until last night."

"One for the books, my brother," Gabe said. "I've seen explosives stall like that—mortars and grenades especially."

Larry took a sheet of paper from his pocket, unfolded it and read:

"The device was cheaply put together. They made it with aluminum wires that shrunk in the freeze last night from the icy hail storm. Condensation inside the device apparently froze and shorted it out when the vehicle heated up and melted it. A charge imbalance in the static electricity caused a short in the device—"

Larry set the paper on the table, took his reading glasses off.

"—boom," he said.

"I'll be damned," Gabe said. "Hail caused it to go off."

"Does Peck know anything about this?"

"No, but he knows he can come back. Lily Cup called Sasha," Larry said.

"Can you take me to a dealer?" Gabe asked.

"Dealer?"

"I want to get him a new pickup."

"After breakfast, of course, brother."

"Heard anything from Peck?" Gabe asked.

"He'll be in town this afternoon. He's at his momma's," Larry said.

"When the world was young and I was young, I can remember seventeen- and eighteen-year-old boys were bombing Berlin, winning a world war. Today, thirty is the new eighteen—but that young man, our Peck, early twenties is such an example for the world."

"You're a wise man, brother Gabe."

"I've been around, ya know?"

"*Scent of a Woman*—1992," Larry said.

"That was before your time, brother," Gabe said.

"I'm older than you think," Larry said. "And I'm a big movie fan of anything army—that one, *Patton*, you name 'em. I've seen them plenty."

"Hooo haaa!" Gabe howled in his best Lieutenant Colonel Frank Slade (*Al Pacino*) voice. He held his coffee mug up for another pour.

As Larry and Gabe stepped out of the Silver Whistle Café, Sasha awoke, opened her eyes, smiled and whispered in Peck's ear.

"*Qu'est-ce qui sent si bon, Peck?*" ("What smells so good, Peck?")

"*Laissez les bons temps rouler,*" Peck said. ("Let the good times roll.")

Peck lifted up and rested on his elbow, looking into Sasha's eyes as she straddled his midriff.

"That sweet smell is bell pepper, an 'onyon, bébé and some celery, dass for true."

"The Holy Trinity," Sasha said.

"Bait Man Alex, he's crab boiling, I bet," Peck said.

Peck started to lift Sasha's thigh to get up. Sasha took his face in hand and looked in his eyes.

"Thanks for last night, Peck. I was so scared."

Peck took the hint and leaned in.

"You okay now, bébé?" Peck whispered.

"You saved my life, big guy—then you made me feel good all night—no nightmares. But I'm still scared—for you. What kind of people—?"

They kissed—their first grown-up kiss.

"Larry say we can go home, cher?"

"He really said it—well Lily Cup said it, but Larry needs you in N'Orleans at one-thirty—he didn't tell me why."

"Let's go pass a good time. We suck some tails and eat us some Amite River crab," Peck said.

Cozy warm, both wearing Peck's boxer briefs, Peck and Sasha stepped through the curtain into the saloon where Bait Man Alex, his wife, and Mamma sat. A kettle filled with boiled crab and crawfish was in the center of the table. Another full kettle rested on top of the wood stove.

"Seventy-two crabs, nineteen crawfish, Peck," Bait man Alex said.

"Them crabs was hungry for your chicken necks," Peck mused. "Crawfish come in to hide from crawfish snakes."

"A good haul, Peck—so good I left the traps out."

"You're a good frien'," Peck said.

Sasha and Peck pulled up chairs and sat at the table.

"It was the full moon," Sasha said.

Peck handed her a crab cracker.

"I could eat a horse," Sasha said.

"If your wrist hurts, bébé, I'll crack 'em for you."

"You did good, Mamma—you raised this boy proper," Sasha said.

She leaned and kissed Mamma on a cheek.

8.

IT WAS A QUIET DRIVE FROM MAMMA'S houseboat on the canal to New Orleans. The city skyline was coming into view when Sasha's iPhone rang.

"Hey," Sasha said.

"Where you at, baby cakes?" Lily Cup asked.

"On our way—Metairie just ahead."

"Peck's phone is off—any reason?" Lily Cup asked.

Sasha leaned on the console.

"Your iPhone's off Peck."

"Ah *oui*. I know—"

"Battery dead?"

"Nah-nah—it's okay."

"He knows it's off," Sasha said. "How're the roads?"

"Seventy-four degrees." Lily Cup said. "See you at the house."

Sasha leaned on the console. "Peck, why is your phone off?"

"I need to concentrate on the bomb and what happened, cher. No distractions."

"He's thinking about last night," Sasha whispered.

"So, he hasn't called her," Lily Cup said.

"My guess is no."

Lily Cup whispered as if hinting to Sasha to have him call and tell Millie what happened—at least so she could hear his voice.

"We were certain you two were dead. I fainted at Charlie's when they told me you were outside with Peck," Lily Cup said.

"You're serious, aren't you? I mean this is not a—"

"I thought I'd never forgive Larry for not telling us you were okay until after it was too late."

"Did he tell you why?"

"All he said was an attempted murder scene is tight lipped—gathering evidence—not spilling clues. He's right, of course—but we were destroyed thinking you and—"

"He could have gotten word to you somehow."

The call ended.

"Peck, Larry wants to see you for something. Drive to Lily Cup's—he's waiting. I'll drive home from there."

It was a mile before Sasha spoke again.

"Peck, you should call Millie."

Peck faced forward. His eyes on the road as if he was counting the broken lane markings in a trance. He glanced at his iPhone, as if tempted to turn it on. He didn't. Neither spoke until he pulled the Bentley in front of Lily Cup's house. He left it running, but in *Park*. He unbuckled and turned in his seat. He watched a boy on a bicycle ride by. He caught Sasha's eye.

"There was this time, cher."

He paused in thought.

"I love that girl—but I can't tell you what happened. You're going to have to trust me, I'm doing right—and I'm wrenched about it, not being with her, but I have to do it."

Sasha didn't respond—she sat and waited.

Peck turned his phone on, waited for it to light up and called Millie.

"Peck! Are you okay?" Millie asked.

"I'm fine, bébé—wanted to tell you I'm okay."

"Lily Cup called me. I've been reading the Bible."

"Millie—there's something I want to say, can you give me a minute to—how you say—gather my thoughts?"

"*But if we hope for what we do not see, we wait for it with patience*," Millie said. "It's from the Bible."

Peck went on to explain what happened and how it happened—and that yes, he and Sasha were lucky to be alive. He explained his knack for tracking he learned in the swamps made him a good investigator and he knew there were risks. He reminded her of the risks she took with him the time they tracked the knife man highway robber when they first met.

"I'm losing you, aren't I, Peck?"

"But cher, with me doing investigations—"

"That's an excuse, Peck. You were hiding from alligators when you were five. You've climbed cypress trees when you were nine to hide from a man who dragged you as gator bait behind his boat. You've supported yourself since you were a child by fishing and selling fish and sharpening blades and mowing lawns. You've washed windows for cans of chicory and bottles of cinnamon. I fell in love with that man—the man who couldn't read or write. I fell in love with him the day he wouldn't take no for an answer from the bus driver and made him stop the bus to let him off so he could run a mile just to bring me my baby doll, Charlie, a doll I've had since I was four years old—a doll a girl he hardly knew left on the bus. That man who got in Tulane night school a year after he taught himself to read."

Peck didn't respond.

"*The Lord giveth and the Lord taketh away*," Millie said.

"What are you saying, cher?"

"You're a free spirit, Peck. I love you too much to tie you down. I'm setting you free."

"So, you understand, Millie? But how—?"

"I knew it this morning when Lily Cup called me at 3:30 and you hadn't already called me. If things were right between us, nothing would have stopped you from calling me when it happened—your pickup blowing up."

Peck didn't respond.

"Peck, let's take a break. I'll work on my Masters."

"For true. Bébé? Not talking marriage and babies?"

"A girl knows these things Peck. I felt it coming. Let's take a break. You're as free as a bird. We both are."

"For true? You're okay with it?"

"I know you go to Baton Rouge, Peck. I know you see Audrey for a reading, but I know what Elizabeth means to you. Don't change your life for me. Whether we ever get back together and raise chickens and crawfish or we never meet again and you investigate on your own, you'll always be in my heart. Now, as you would say, Peck—pass you a good time."

"You're a special woman, Millie—dass for true."

"You're a special man, Boudreaux Clemont Finch. Maybe I'll see you on a bus someday."

Peck smiled.

"Ciao, Peck."

The call ended.

"You okay, Peck?" Sasha asked.

Peck didn't respond.

Sasha leaned over and kissed him on the cheek.

"You're a good man, Peck."

Peck gazed through the windshield.

"Thanks for last night, Peck—"

"Ah *oui*, cher."

"Go in, see what Larry wants. I'm going home."

A car pulled beside the Bentley and the horn honked. It was Larry, his window down. Peck lowered his window.

"Hop in, we have stops to make," Larry said.

Sasha got out and walked around to the driver's side of the Bentley.

"Hey, Larry."

"Hey Sasha—hell of a night, eh? How's the wrist?"

"It's fine. Slept like a baby. Peck's amazing."

"He's something else, he surely is," Larry said.

Through the window, Sasha handed Larry a shopping bag holding her ravaged Givenchy and broken Louboutin heels.

"You two going to the station, Larry?"

"First stop—yes."

"Can you drop this at Goodwill? Put it in their bin. It'll be Mardi Gras fun for somebody."

"Pretty lady—I'm ordering the gang to be at Charlie's tonight—we're going to dance jazz all night if that's what it takes to put this behind us. The scene's been scrubbed. The only memories of that alley and of Frenchman Street I want us to have are the sweet sounds of jazz, the wail of the blues and us boys watching ladies move their stuff."

"Larry lifted the sack.

"These your things?"

"Yep."

"Pretty torn up?"

Sasha pursed her lips.

"Saks Fifth Avenue is open, pretty lady—why don't you go in the house, grab some of Lily Cup's chicory—and you two go do some damage at Saks."

"Sounds like a plan," Sasha said.

"See you tonight," Larry said.

Larry drove off with Peck.

9.

LARRY AND PECK stepped into the precinct.

"Peck, that third room down the hall, it's for interrogation. Grab a seat—we're going to talk about last night. I'll bring coffee. You want a roll? A donut?"

"Coffee's good, frien'."

Peck was sitting when Larry came in the room. Larry had two coffees in hand and a long, flat piece of steel looking like a yardstick under his arm. He sat and handed Peck a coffee.

"Was this in your pickup, Peck?"

He slid it across the table.

"Nah-nah," Peck said.

"You've never seen it before?"

"Nah-nah."

"It's important we try to recreate last night—we need to see if your subconscious is holding something you may have seen or heard. Can you work with me, son?"

"Let's do it," Peck said.

"Do you remember leaving Charlie's?"

"Ah *oui*. I wanted to pick up the—how you say—tab, and I ax Charlie could I pay for the table when I come back another time. He tol' me yes."

"Then you left?"

"First we watched Sasha walking to the ladies' room."

"She's something to watch," Larry said.

"Ah *oui*—bodacious, Charlie called her."

"Then you left?"

"Ah *oui*."

"As you walked out what were you looking at?"

"I was watching for ice in the alley, then on Frenchman Street, trying not to slip."

"You made it to Frenchman Street—then what?"

"I thought I saw something moving near my truck, and I was watching, but that's when the wind gusted good and ice come off the live oak and purdy much covered everything around me—how you say, distracting me—and that's when Sasha grabbed my arm."

"Sasha went out with you?"

"Nah-nah, Sasha come out to give me my phone. I left it on the bar, talking to Charlie."

"But you did see a man by your truck?"

"I saw something. It was on the other side of the pickup—but only for a second, Larry—could have been a man or a woman."

"What next?"

"Sasha was freezing. I gave her my leather coat and zipped her up. I remember she held on my arm tight to keep from slipping. That's when my pickup blew up—big as hell, Larry. I remember pushing her to the ground—"

"To the ground or into the bushes?"

"Ah *oui*—into the bushes—"

"And you jumped on her."

"Nah-nah."

"You didn't jump on her?"

"Nah-nah, Larry—there was another explosion that throwed me. It hit me and I flew sideways and landed on her—knocked the wind out of her."

"We heard the second explosion."

"My guess, Larry—the gas tank."

"You said you thought you saw something moving by your pickup—the wind blows ice from trees—Sasha grabs your arm—the bomb explodes and you push her down, the pickup explodes again and you land on her in the bushes—that about it?"

"Don't forget when Sasha grabs my arm that's when I took my jacket off and put it on her—I remember that."

"That jacket saved her from being badly hurt."

"It was cold, bébé. I did it without thinkin'."

Larry picked up the sheath of flat steel.

"Larry, I remember the side mirror from my pickup dropped out of the sky. It was like a stage lamp dropping down in a murder mystery play I saw in Baton Rouge with Elizabeth. It landed on Sasha's shoe that had come off when I pushed her. I heard it then I turned my head to see what the clunk was. I told Sasha to be quiet, don't talk. I remember her axing are we going to die—and I touched her lips with my finger signaling not to speak. We lay until I saw you."

"Got it, Peck. Had to be a frightening moment for both of you. It's over and done with, Peck. There won't be any reprisals. We know who did it and when." Larry pulled papers from his pocket and read from them aloud.

"Forensics traced a shipping tracking number glued on the casing of the device."

"Didn't it burn up, Larry?"

"It was attached to the tailpipe."

"Ah."

"Peck, it was delivered into Storyville months ago."

"Storyville?"

"Peck, the mechanism was shipped to your friend, dollar sign-tattooed pimp man you handled months ago."

Peck had killed the sex trafficking pimp man months ago, and Larry chose to cover it up.

"This doesn't leave this room, but with him long gone, we feel you're safe—"

"And it blows up now, Larry? Why, you think?"

"They're calling it a delayed anomaly of science that made it spark in the freeze. I haven't told anyone about this, Peck … I don't want them to know what you and I know about that pimp and his address."

"Thanks, frien'."

"Now let's get out of here."

They left the precinct, walking down the steps.

"Follow me, Peck."

"Hanh?"

Larry handed Peck a key fob and pointed to a new pickup parked on the street.

"Gabe tried to get you the khaki color you had. Will black do?" Larry asked.

"You and Gabe do this, frien'?"

"Gabe and your insurance."

"I love it, dass for true. Thanks, frien'."

"Jump in and follow me, Peck."

"Where we going cher?"

"To the morgue."

"Hanh?"

"We have an appointment with a coroner."

10.

EYEING LARRY AND PECK walking into the morgue's cold room, Coroner O'Sullivan lifted his face shield, pulled off rubber gloves and stepped over.

"Chris O'Sullivan here, you must be Peck. Good to meet you."

"I come with the Lieutenant here—not sure why," Peck said.

"He didn't tell you?"

"Nah-nah."

"We need to see if you can identify a body. May I call you Peck?"

"Ah *oui*, Peck is good. What body? Larry?"

"I didn't want to spoil your drive in a new pickup, son. How'd she ride?"

"She's a beauty."

Chris led them to a table with a naked white male cadaver on it. A plastic sheet covered the torso where the coroner was performing the autopsy. The skin on the face was missing and the skeletal face bones charred black. A wire on one toe held an identification tag.

"Are you able to identify this man?" Chris asked.

"Nah-nah," Peck said.

Chris handed Peck photos of the corpse wearing an expensive tuxedo.

"Maybe these pictures will help," Chris said.

"I don't know him, Chris," Peck said. "Sorry."

"Lieutenant, Rick Clancy called you about the bomb, right?" Chris asked.

"He did. Told me the bomb dated back several months. He faxed me his findings—"

"Did you read them?" Chris asked.

"I did. Freeze from the hail storm, condensation build up and faulty aluminum wiring that set it off."

"Does it make sense to you. Lieutenant?"

"It absolutely makes sense to me."

"Well now they're saying, because of the way this man was dressed, he was likely on his way to work at a club or restaurant—perhaps a musician or Maître-d or something like that. They're thinking it's a case of a man being in the wrong place at the wrong time."

He paused.

"But I'm not buying it," Chris said.

"I'm not buying it either," Larry said.

Peck spoke up. "Nah-nah—I'm—how you say—not buying it too."

"Imagine that," Larry said.

"Great minds?" Chris asked.

"Triple crown," Larry said. "Ring-a-ding-ding."

"Who goes first, Lieutenant?" Chris asked.

"Talk to me, Chris."

"Lieutenant, if this man was just walking by the pickup on his way to work—he would have been charred, of course—seems to me he might even have been blown into a yard or someplace away from the pickup. But I'm pretty certain the skin on his face wouldn't be burned completely off, almost as if he stuck his head in a microwave. Your turn, Lieutenant."

"There's a reason *charbroiled* here was not blown back into a yard—a reason his face is missing."

Larry held up the sheath of steel.

"Here's proof. A little something forensics missed. It was next to the curb covered in ice."

"What is it, Lieutenant?" Chris asked.

"Gentlemen, it's an access tool—popularly called a 'Slim Jim.' Standard with fire departments, car thieves, bad boys—you know, the regulars."

"You found that by the body?" Peck asked.

"It was under the body, buried under a layer of ice. He dropped it because he didn't need it anymore. He had the door open. He wasn't blown back onto a lawn because he was maybe holding onto a seatbelt to pull himself in—or maybe he was gripping the door handle. That's why he didn't fly back into a yard. His face is missing because the bomb was likely in the console or the glove box and exploded just as he stuck his head inside."

"So, your theory is he was a car thief stealing the vehicle, Lieutenant?" Chris asked.

"Stealing, burglarizing—not sure which."

"Prove the bomb was inside the car and not under the car and on a frame, Lieutenant."

"I think I proved it this morning over breakfast, reading Clancy's forensic report on the bomb."

"Care to share?"

"Peck—spilled anything in your console recently?" Larry asked.

"Ah *oui*."

"Talk to me."

"Gabe looking for a street map, he tipped a small Styrofoam cup of chicory. He wiped it up purdy good."

"Why do you ask, Lieutenant?" Chris asked.

"Condensation. In a freeze—all freezable parts of a vehicle are likely to freeze, correct?"

"Yes, Lieutenant."

"When a vehicle's engine is started—and the heater and defroster are on, the only area of the vehicle to heat up enough to thaw condensation on faulty wires would be inside the vehicle. The apparatus was on the frame, not near the engine and not inside the vehicle—they've proven that—but my guess is the detonating device and explosive were hidden in a flashlight, a tool kit, something that wouldn't draw attention—sitting in the console or glovebox—men don't examine consoles—men toss, retrieve and mop up spilled drinks—not watching what they're doing."

"You're good, Lieutenant. It's a pleasure watching you think."

"You ain't seen nothing, Chris."

"How's that, Lieutenant?"

"Peck here is our thinker. If you want to see thinking in dark, tight spots, get it from someone who grew up in a swamp poling through alligators and throwing nets—and I don't have a clue what he's thinking."

Larry turned to Peck.

"Son, you've heard our theories—what's yours— why aren't you buying Forensics' theory about this man walking by on his way to work?"

Larry smiled at Chris, nodding toward Peck.

"Talk to us, Peck."

"This man—our gator wasn't walking to work. He was coming home from work."

"How you figure, son?" Larry asked.

"A gator ain't going to risk messing up an expensive tuxedo stealing a pickup—he'd have to look nice at work. He was goin' home from work."

Larry and Chris nodded.

"They's two kinds of gators, frien'. The gator that waits for—how you say—unsuspecting prey to come by. All you see is eyes and snout—looks like a rock— no motion. Then the prowler. Gator can do twenty miles an hour in a swamp—thirty-five on land. Congregations, that's a lot of gators out hunting, don't stop until they find food—when they do, they can jump five, maybe six feet to grab it … *chomp*."

Peck pointed at the cadaver.

"That gator wasn't moving last night, friens', he was lying in wait—other side of my pickup. Problem with that is—nothing to wait for. The pickup was setting there."

"You've seen him, Peck—and you've seen pictures. What's on your mind?" Larry asked.

"Men don't steal pickups in tuxedos, Larry."

"What's it saying to you, Peck?"

"Maybe waiting for me—did he have a gun?"

"No firearms," Chris said.

"Maybe thinking about stealing the truck. It was empty and it was running."

"Opportunity," Larry said.

"But he wasn't moving when I saw him—maybe he had second thoughts."

"What's that say to you Peck? His having second thoughts?" Larry asked.

"Somebody was making him steal it, cher."

"You think because he paused, it was a conscience pause—you think he was being forced to do something he would never do on his own?" Chris asked.

"Ah *oui*."

"He jimmied open the door, Peck," Larry said.

"He's not a car thief, bébé," Peck said. "Somebody making him do it."

"What makes you so sure, son?" Larry asked.

"A car thief doesn't drop his tools and let 'em get covered by ice."

"I can buy that," Larry said.

"I can too, Lieutenant," Chris said.

"He was in a tuxedo, so he was coming from work, knowing he had to steal a truck or car. If my pickup wasn't running, he might could have stolen some other car, some other time."

"Dead on, Peck," Larry said. "If that's how it went down, it's a murder."

"Do you know who he is, Chris?" Peck asked.

"Anthony Bergeron, Peck."

Chris handed him the corpse's identification.

"Mr. Bergeron had no record of arrests—before this past week. He was a musician—played the piano. Lived in a shotgun he and his wife own on Magazine Street."

"What do you mean before this past week?" Peck asked. "How do you know about the shotgun?"

"He and a friend were held overnight for suspicion of drug trafficking in an alley in the French Quarter," Chris said. "They were arraigned the next morning—he pled not guilty. His friend pled guilty—which implicated him."

"And the shotgun?" Peck asked.

"Two receipts in his wallet for paint and brushes. They have his address on them—it's a shotgun on Magazine Street."

"The autopsy come up with anything, Chris?" Larry asked.

"He was a scotch drinker—Italian sausage fan—but no signs of drugs or marijuana in his blood, his lungs or in his stomach."

"This sound like a setup, Chris?" Larry asked.

"The judge set bail for his friend but ordered our cadaver here to be held, saying he was a risk for disappearing. Strange as it may sound, that's apparently when he disappeared. You tell me, Lieutenant."

Chris held a Bergeron family picture up for Peck.

"This was folded in his wallet. Does this look like a pusher to you, Peck? He's married—two kids, a baby named Ally and a ten-year-old daughter, Bernadette. His wife is a substitute pre-school teacher and a legal assistant and this here is his streetcar Jazzy pass. They don't own a vehicle. A law-abiding, working-class native N'Orleans citizen just a few blocks away from where he'd catch his streetcar home."

"Chris," Peck started. "They're Cajun French—Bergeron. Any papers or notes in his pockets or wallet written in French?"

"Nothing," Chris said.

"Have the next of kin been notified?" Larry asked.

"Homicide or murders under investigation—that'd be your purview, Lieutenant."

"Got to be a reason this man was doing something he had to think twice about doing, Larry," Peck said.

"What's going on in your mind, son?" Larry asked.

"This whole thing smells—dass for true. It needs tracking. Questions need answering."

"You ready for the task, son?"

"Can I, Larry?"

"You're a private investigator, Peck—a citizen volunteer. You're not a deputy, son."

"I know."

"Go for it. You've got new wheels—and a full tank—you'll get mileage and a *per diem*—keep records and keep me posted, son."

"I'm impressed with him, Lieutenant," Chris said.

"Give me three days, Larry," Peck said.

"Why do you think, three days, Peck?" Chris asked.

"Watch this, Chris," Larry said. "Peck, where's your first stop going to be—early Mass at the Basilica in the morning?"

"Ah *oui*," Peck said.

"Chris, our man Boudreaux Clemont here has a routine for tracking, a discipline—he's a maestro. It's like he's conducting a symphony. You ain't seen nothing yet."

Larry's phone rang.

"Talk to me."

"Lieutenant, this is Downs. You asked me to call you about robberies."

"I asked you to call about anything suspicious," Larry said.

"We have a jewelry store robbery yesterday on Maple Street."

"Weapons used?"

"No weapons. All we know is it was a grab and run, Lieutenant."

"Good work, Downs. Text that store's address to Peck. I want his eyes on it first."

"Will do, sir."

The call ended.

"Peck, check your texts for an address from Officer Downs. A robbery on Maple Street—a jewelry store. I want you to check it out now, get some preliminaries, and then get right back on this case."

"Yes, sir."

Peck left the morgue.

11.

PECK PULLED IN FRONT of the jewelry store on Maple Street. He parked and called Larry.

"Larry, I'm here."

"Check it out, son."

"I'll need you to call them and tell them who I am, Larry. I don't have a badge."

"Officer Downs is our point man on that robbery. I'll give him a call."

"Okay."

"Hold on."

"Okay."

Peck turned his pickup off. He waited.

"Peck?"

"Yes?"

"There's a Paul Robert waiting for you inside. Help yourself."

"Thanks, frien'."

Peck went into the store.

"Mr. Paul Robert, was it a man or a woman who robbed your store?"

"Call me Paul. I believe it was a man, a white man."

"You are sure?"

"He had a hoody pulled nearly closed. Only an eye could be seen. I could see his wrists just above the gloves he wore."

"You could tell he was a man by the wrists?"

"Actually, I couldn't. Now I'm not certain. I just assumed it was a man."

"Did the robber have a weapon? A gun or knife?"

"Whoever it was didn't brandish a weapon, if that's what you're asking."

Peck looked up the definition of *brandish* on his iPhone.

"Ah *oui*. That's what I was asking."

"Dashed in, ran right to a customer who was holding up a ring. The robber must have seen the gem through the window. She had a glass and was looking at its clarity. We only carry the best. Since 1959."

"Did you see him or her approach her?"

"I did. He ran to her, grabbed the ring and dashed out—that fast. I really think this was a man. I don't know, the shoulders or something."

"The man grabbed the ring from her hand?"

"Yes. Frightened her."

"Were there other customers in the store when this happened?"

Paul Robert looked over at a sales girl.

"Lou Ann, do you recall if there were other customers here when that man ran in?"

"Mrs. Lederman was here, Paul. We were sizing her gold watch band."

"Mr. Finch, there was one other customer here, a Mrs. Lederman … you heard."

"I wonder, Mr. Robert. Did this man who run in here—did he run over to Mrs. Lederman too?"

"Lou Ann?" Paul Robert asked.

"He didn't. He made a dash directly to the customer and then ran out of the store," Lou Ann said. "I thought he must know her, he ran to her so directly."

"Interesting. Did the lady appear to recognize the man?"

"It all happened so fast, I don't think she even saw him. She was looking through the glass at the gem," Lou Ann said.

"Mr. Robert, can I ax who the lady was in case I need to talk to her?"

"Absolutely not. We would never compromise our customer's safety by disclosing names. Absolutely not."

"You told me about Mrs. Lederman, Mr. Robert."

"Mrs. Lederman wasn't buying diamonds."

"Can I see your surveillance tape?"

"It's a DVD disk. I can't play it here but I can give it to you. Will that do?"

"That will do fine. Thanks."

Peck got the disk and left the store. He put it in his glove box and drove to the precinct. He went inside to the sergeant at the desk.

"Sergeant, can I ax if you have a machine to play a surveillance disk I got?"

"We do. I'll see that it's set up for you."

"That machine—is it hard to work?"

"Just flip a switch, turn a knob."

He was given what looked like a laptop that would read the disc and he went down the hall to his interrogation room. He plugged the machine in, inserted the disc and sat back. The screen showed the jewelry store from the ceiling of the back wall. Two silhouettes of people standing in the store could be seen, but because of the sun coming in through the windows behind them, they were not recognizable. A person in a sweat suit and hoody was clearly visible entering the store, running to the one silhouette of a person, grabbing something from her, then turning and running out.

Peck didn't know how to start it again so his solution was to remove the disc and put it in the machine again. The disc just replayed the robbery. Peck stood and left the machine and walked to the desk sergeant.

"How you all are, Sergeant?"

"Couldn't be better, friend—how's your day going?"

"Tell you the truth, Sergeant, I need me somebody smart with how you say—electronics—like the machine in there."

"It's not all that difficult," the sergeant said.

"I was thinking a kid who plays those video games. I see them in stores playing them so good, Sergeant."

"Let me call upstairs, friend. I have an idea. Give me a second."

The sergeant lifted his desk phone and made a call.

"Ms. Knapp, is your niece in the building?"

"Maizie?"

"Yes ma'am, Maizie—is she still in the building?"

"She is—at a borrowed desk doing her homework, why are you asking, Sergeant?"

"Is she good with computers?"

"She's a whiz with computers."

"There's a private detective in Interrogation Room Three that needs a hand with a computer and a surveillance disc."

"Just a second, Sergeant. I'll ask," Mrs. Knapp said.

A few minutes later she was back on the line:

"Sergeant, Maizie is on her way down. She'll be happy to help."

The sergeant looked up at Peck and smiled. "I'll send her to number three when she gets here," he said.

"Thanks, frien'."

Peck had pulled a seat up to the computer on the table when there was a knock on the door.

"Come in, are you the Maizie I heard about?"

"I'm Maizie. You need help with a computer?"

"My name is Boudreaux Clemont Finch, but everybody calls me Peck."

"Hi Peck."

"Here's the story, Maizie—when it comes to machines like this, I am not so good. Fact is, I'm bad. I can't pay you much, but can you run it for me?"

"I don't want money. Can I write a paper for school about the experience?"

"Writing a paper would be so good, bébé. I'd like to read it, for true."

Maizie stepped over to the machine and sat down. Peck pulled a chair behind her to watch the screen over her shoulder.

"What are you trying to do?" Maizie asked.

"Play the video and keep playing it," Peck said.

"Playing it is simple," Maizie said.

She inserted the disc and sat back as it played.

"There," she said.

"Ah *oui*, that's good," Peck said. "But is there any way you can—how you say—slow the movie down?"

"You mean slo-mo?" Maizie asked.

"Is that what you call it?"

"Yes."

"Can you do that?"

"Sure. How slow do you want it?"

"Slo-mo it like purdy slow and we'll see. If I need it slower, I'll ax, okay?"

"No problem. What's this person running in the store doing? Hitting or robbing that lady?"

"You can tell it's a lady?" Peck asked.

"Pretty sure, yes."

"How? All I can see is a black—how you say—silhouette," Peck said.

Maizie played the disc again.

"Watch the shoulder," she said.

With a pen she pointed to the silhouette's shoulder.

"What am I looking for?"

"Watch for the dent on the top of that shoulder"

"I don't see it."

"Hold on, I'll slow it down more."

Maizie backed the disc up and found a place to restart.

"Now watch—look for the dent—it's something pressing down on the shoulder."

"I see it—I see it good now—dass for true."

"Good," Maizie said.

"How's a dent make that silhouette a lady though?"

"That dent is from the strap of a purse. That's how I figured it's a lady."

"Some men carry purses, don't they?"

"Not with chain straps they don't," Maizie said.

"You are smart, just like the sergeant said. All that from looking at her shoulder."

"Well, I saw the dent first—but then I confirmed it."

"That's good tracking, Maizie—how did you confirm it?"

"Let me back it up again. I'll show you."

"Okay."

Maizie brought the picture to the spot she wanted and froze it.

"There," she said.

"What are we looking at?"

With a pen Maizie touched the screen.

"See this silver vase—this one here with yellow roses in it, Peck?"

"I can see it."

"It's tiny but if you look closely, you can see the reflection of the C's—that's a Chanel handbag. When I saw the dent, that's why I looked around and saw this."

"Well, I'll be. You should be in forensics," Peck said. "You can teach them some things, for sure."

"Was that person robbing the store?" Maizie asked.

"We think so—can you maybe do me something, Maizie?"

"I'll try. What?"

"Have you ever been in a swamp in a pirogue?"

"I don't know what a pirogue is, but I've seen swamps. Why?"

"A pirogue is a small boat. Sometimes carved out of a log of wood. With a pole you stand in it and push your way through a swamp to see gators and see where the best place to throw a net would be."

"To catch an alligator with a net? That sounds dangerous."

"Nah-nah—not a gator, but to see where the crawfish snakes are waiting to go under. That's where crawfish are on the bottom and the biggest fish will be under the water. They eat 'em too—crawfish."

"I don't think I understand your point, Peck."

"I'm looking for something on this disc, bébé."

"Like what?"

"I'm looking to see if that person in the sweatsuit was alone."

"Looked alone to me. How can you tell?"

"Do that slo-mo thing and just keep doing it—and I'll keep watching whoever it is we think is robbing the store, Maizie. We're thinking the lady with the—how you say—Chanel bag, was looking at a diamond that was grabbed."

Maizie set the disc in slo-mo and Peck leaned into the screen and watched.

"Again," Peck said.

It repeated.

"Again," Peck said.

It repeated six times.

"Okay, Maizie. Enough."

"Did you find what you wanted?"

"I surely did—dass for true. That robber's not alone."

"What? Where?" Maizie asked.

"Wanna see it?"

"Yes, please. This is so good."

"Play it again, three times—and these times watch for a van that comes from the left and passes in front of the store."

Maizie replayed the disc.

"You're right, it is a van," Maizie said.

"I see two things about the van that make me suspicious," Peck said.

"Two things?"

"See how slow the van is driving—traffic is passing it by."

"Yes, I can see that," Maizie said.

"Now watch that the robber walks to the right at the same speed as the van driving by."

"You're right," Maizie said. "I totally see it."

"And there's a sign on the side of the van," Peck said. "Can you stop the picture so we maybe can read the sign?"

Maizie obliged.

"It's blurry here. The sign was painted over, but I can see some letters," Maizie said.

Peck stood up.

"Thank you for your help, frien'. You are such a smart detective. I've got things to do now and want all what you showed me sink into my pea brain."

"Peck, if I promise not to lose it, can I take this disc home and experiment with it? I want to watch it a bunch of times like you did and see what I can see. May I?"

"I'll need it back."

"I'll be here tomorrow. I promise I'll bring it back."

"Okay, take it. I'll be here tomorrow too. I'll ax the desk sergeant to call you. You can bring it down then."

Maizie left with the disc. Peck returned the machine to the desk sergeant.

"Thank you for everything, Sergeant."

"All in a day's work, son."

Peck's phone rang.

"Larry?" Peck asked.

"Find anything on the robbery, son?"

"Some things, Larry. I did."

"Been to Magazine Street yet?"

"The Bergeron's?

"Yes—to tell the widow about our dead man?"

"In the morning, Larry. I need to clear my head about what I'm piling in it."

"Peck, that's the world we live in, son. We pile it up like dirty laundry and then—*poof*—one day it all makes sense—and it all comes clean in the wash."

"If dass for true, Larry, I'll be a happy man."

The call ended.

Later that day, Peck's phone rang.

"Hello?"

"Peck, this is the night desk sergeant."

"Yes sir," Peck said.

"I took a message for you, and when I checked with Lieutenant Gaines, he said to call you and give it to you."

"Thanks, Sergeant."

"The message is that a Maizie's aunt called. She said that Maizie did some work on a project she was helping you with on a computer up in forensics and that she's holding some things Maizie has for you."

"Okay."

"She told me Maizie thinks she'll be here in the morning until noon—some teacher's conference or something—but in case she isn't coming in, her aunt will bring a package down and leave it with the daytime desk sergeant when she comes in. She has a few stops to make before coming in."

"What package?" Peck asked.

"Her aunt has some pictures or something Maizie printed out for you. If Maizie can't come in, the aunt will bring them when she's finished her errands."

"Thanks, Sergeant. If she calls again, tell her I'm going to early Mass tomorrow but I'll be in after."

"Will do, Mr. Finch."

12.

PECK'S FIRST STOP THE NEXT MORNING, was the Basilica and early Mass. He was distracted, and he knelt with cupped prayerful hands over his mouth whispering into them, paying little attention to the Mass.

"God, I need your help special this time. I've got to go tell a lady her husband is dead, God. I know I ask a lot and you busy enough already, dass for true. But God there's a man dead and he sure enough was a good daddy and a loving husband and now Larry and Mr. O'Sullivan are axin' can I find who'd hurt a daddy."

Peck stood and walked to the altar rail and accepted communion from Father McBride. He blessed himself and walked back to the candles. He pushed some folded bills into the donation slot and lighted three.

"I know these votive candles ain't much, Mr. Bergeron—what happened to you and all. I know some folks will be mighty hurt and sad when they see you're gone and not coming back. Maybe the candles will keep you alive in hearts and maybe remind God to light my way to finding out what happened and why you're dead and not me. *And God, I've got to go tell the momma what happened. Please help me."*

Peck touched the Holy water, blessed himself with the sign of the cross and left the church.

13.

"THANKS FOR COMING down, Maizie. Last night the desk sergeant wasn't sure you'd be in. I'm glad you could come. There's someplace I have to go but I came in to see what you have. Your aunt said you used the computers upstairs and maybe found things on the disc?" Peck asked.

Maizie opened a notebook to a page with a star drawn on the top.

"Peck, can I tell you what I found first? If that's okay with you then I can show you on the disc."

"That'll be good," Peck said.

"I have a list I printed out, so bear with me. Number one—that person who ran into the jewelry store didn't rob it."

"Hahn?"

"And that person didn't rob that lady, either."

"Hanh?" Peck asked.

"I'll explain in a minute."

"*Aye yi-yi*," Peck mumbled.

"Number two—I can tell some of the license plate number. Not all of it but some.

"This is so good, bébé. Anything else?"

"Yes. Number three—the person that ran in has a rectangular—looks like onyx—ring on one finger."

"Was it like his wedding ring, you think, Maizie?"

"I don't know, Peck, and I can't tell if it is a man's or a woman's ring."

"For true?"

"I'm just not sure. With that hooded sweatshirt hanging loose and not showing hips or waist, I couldn't tell. I show the ring just in case a jeweler can tell if it's a man's ring or a women's ring, but my pictures of the hand never show the fingers, only fists."

"Good thinking, bébé."

"Thank you."

"You say that person didn't rob the store, show me," Peck said.

Maizie set up the laptop and inserted the disc. She lifted a manilla envelope. From it she pulled several printouts of blown-up jpegs she had lifted from the screen.

"Peck, I have four close-up pictures of the van, but here I have four pictures of that person in the sweat suit approaching the woman. Look at these ones in order."

Maizie set them side by side on the table.

"What am I looking at, Maizie?"

"These are printout closeups of what you think is the robber's hand reaching out near the lady's face."

"I see, yes," Peck said.

"There are four pictures of the hand getting closer and closer to the lady's face—"

"I can see that," Peck said.

"—and this last one—here—is the very last image of the hand before it was pulled back."

"Before the robber's hand was pulled back?"

"It's what the camera caught. It recorded exactly when the hand stopped its forward motion and started to be pulled back."

"Looks like there was no contact," Peck said.

"That hand didn't grab anything or take anything," Maizie said.

"*Aye yi-yi.*"

"That person ran in, reached for air, almost like the hand was going to hit the lady—grabbed nothing, hit nothing and then turned and ran out."

Peck jumped up.

"It's almost spooky," Maizie said.

"This is so good, Maizie. A real mystery. Was Mr. Paul Robert lying to me?"

"Did I do all right?"

"You did so good, bébé. I have to be someplace. I have to go now."

"Let my aunt know if you ever need anything."

"I will. Thank you so much."

14.

PECK DROVE TO MAGAZINE STREET and parked his new pickup around the corner, a block away from the shotgun house of the dead man burned in the explosion.

As he would when entering any new bayou, the tracker in Peck instinctively took the long way around through the neighborhood—giving him time to track, to take in the culture of the surrounds. He knew Carencro and he knew Baton Rouge like the back of his hand. In New Orleans he knew the French Quarter, a few blocks of Frenchman Street, Storeyville, routes to Sasha's, Lily Cup's—how to get to classes at Tulane night school and not much else. As he walked, he tracked people's movements, he listened for sounds. This neighborhood wasn't a Big Easy caricature; it was a living part of real New Orleans life—shops and restaurants for locals, not overrun with tourists. The shotgun house was freshly painted, but Peck paused in his tracks to study it. Something about it bothered him. The outside shutters being closed during daylight hours in a city that celebrated sunlight gave Peck a sense of something not being right.

The wrought iron gate latch in front of the house was tight. It required a fist bump to open. With the sounds of metal on metal the curtain in the front door glass was pulled aside—and quickly closed. He stepped up. Inside he could hear the wails of a baby as if shrieking in terror. He knocked on the door. There was no response. The baby shrieked. He knocked again.

"Mrs. Bergeron?"

No response.

"Mrs. Bergeron, Are you home?"

No answer.

He knocked again.

The baby crying stopped.

"Mrs. Bergeron?"

No response.

"Bernadette, are you in there?"

No response.

"Bernadette, j'ai des nouvelles de ton père. Votre mère dort-elle? Pouvez-vous la réveiller s'il vous plaît?" ("Bernadette, I have news about your father. Is your mother asleep? Can you wake her please?")

The curtain on the door pulled to the side, revealing the face of a ten-year-old child looking up at Peck in a frozen stare.

"Êtes-vous Bernadette?" ("Are you Bernadette?")

Bernadette nodded her head.

"Mommy's not here," Bernadette said.

The baby began shrieking again.

"Is that baby okay, Bernadette?"

"She's hungry," Bernadette said.

"No food in the house, bébé?"

"Mommy went to the store but didn't come back."

Bernadette started to weep. She rubbed her eyes with the backs of her hands.

"I'm scared," she said.

"How long has your momma been gone?"

"I don't know."

"Today?"

"No."

"Yesterday?

"No."

"Before yesterday?"

The baby screamed.

"Let me in, Bernadette. I'll get you some food. I'll find your momma."

The door opened cautiously. Peck stepped in the house. His face wrinkled at the smell of urine in the air. The baby was standing in the crib, her face red from screaming, arms outstretched as if she was begging to be picked up.

Peck lifted her. She was soaking wet. He held her in his arms with little regard for the wet, soiled, diaper. Peck was chained under a porch when he was three and four—he knew the importance of being held—and what this child needed even more than food was to be held.

"You know where the diapers are, Bernadette?"

"Mommy was going to get some."

"Bernadette, can you get me one of your T-shirts? That'll work."

"Okay."

"Get me a towel too, bébé."

Bernadette ran back to her room and came out with a T-shirt and bath towel and handed them to Peck.

"Here."

"Bernadette, fais couler de l'eau dans l'évier—pas trop chaud. Tu sais comment faire ça?" ("Bernadette, run some water in the sink—not too hot. You know how to do that?")

"Oui," Bernadette said. "I know."

"We got to give this baby a bath," Peck said. "She's sore from the diaper mess."

Peck removed the diaper soaked with urine and feces. He set the baby on a newspaper on the floor and put the diaper in a plastic shopping bag he found in the pantry and tied the top. He looked in the refrigerator—it was empty. On the top shelf of the pantry were several cans of chicken noodle soup. He put a pot on the stove, turning a burner on. He opened the cans, poured them in the pot plus two cans of water from the sink.

"When you eat last, bébé?"

"I don't remember."

"Did you know there's cans of soup up here?"

"I couldn't see them. We ate all the crackers on this shelf. I don't know how to open the sardines or the Spam."

"Soup is best for you, bébé—when you have a empty stomach best you start back with soup," Peck said.

He lifted the baby into the sink, gently plunging her up and down, relying on the motion of the bath to clean her bottom. He lifted her out, put the t-shirt on over her head and sat her in the highchair on a folded bath towel.

"Soup's on," Peck said. "Sit at the table, frien'. You want to feed the baby?"

"Peux-tu? J'ai tellement faim." ("Can you? I'm so hungry.")

"Bon appétit," Peck said.

Peck spooned soup into the baby's mouth. Bernadette treated every spoonful as if it was a miracle. She didn't take her eyes off the bowl and the spoon in her hand.

It was just as Peck filled Bernadette's bowl with another helping when the front door slammed open, and a voice screamed.

"What are you doing in our house? Why can't you leave us alone? Where's Anthony?"

She rushed to the table and knelt down hugging the baby and Bernadette.

"I'm so sorry, sweethearts."

"C'est un homme gentil, maman. Ce n'est pas un mauvais homme." ("He's a nice man, Mommy. He's not a bad man.")

"Are you both okay?"

"We're hungry, Mommy. He's a nice man. He found soup and cooked it."

"Who are you?" Mrs. Bergeron asked. "Where's Anthony—their father?"

"Ma'am, I can explain—but these little ones need food in their tummies and we need diapers."

"Where's Anthony?"

"Any store nearby, Mrs. Bergeron?"

"Yes."

"Do you have someone who babysits? I'll take you to a store. We'll talk about Anthony."

"Has something—?" Mrs. Bergeron started.

Peck interrupted her by stern eyes, a shaking of his head and pursed lips—suggesting they not talk in front of the kids.

"Mrs. Bergeron, I'm a private investigator—I work with Lieutenant Larry Gaines. You can call him to check me out if you need to. Can you call a babysitter—let me drive you to a store so you can get things you need? We can talk on the way. Is that good, Mrs. Bergeron?"

"I'll call the sitter."

"Good," Peck said. "I'll get my pickup and come get you out front."

Peck spooned soup to the baby while Mrs. Bergeron made a call.

"Sweet Bernadette and Ally, it was nice meeting you—my name's Peck and one day can I come and take you to Dooky Chase's for chicken and gumbo? You like chicken?"

"Is Peck your real name?" Bernadette asked.

"Mamma named me Boudreaux Clemont, but my friends call me Peck."

"I do," Bernadette said. "I like chicken."

15.

PECK PULLED THE PICKUP to the curb on Magazine Street in front of the Bergeron's shotgun. Mrs. Bergeron opened its door and stood outside, hesitating.

"How do I know I can trust you? I mean you were nice to my kids, but how do I know that's not just an act?"

Peck touched Larry's number on his phone and put it on speaker.

"Talk to me."

Mrs. Bergeron listened intently as Peck spoke into the phone:

"I need you to tell *us* who you are and where you are and *who* I am. I need you to tell us all that."

"My name is Larry Gaines—lieutenant with the New Orleans Police department—my badge is number nine-eight-four. Boudreaux Clemont Finch—we call him Peck—is a private investigator who works with us. He is trustworthy."

"Where's my husband?" Mrs. Bergeron asked. "Why isn't he home? He would never do that. My children were starving."

"That's Mrs. Bergeron, Larry," Peck said. "I'm taking her for groceries."

"Mrs. Bergeron—pick up the phone please? Take it off speaker?"

Peck took it off speaker and handed the phone to Mrs. Bergeron. She put it to her ear.

"Mrs. Bergeron, at approximately ten-seventeen last night a man we believe to be your husband was killed on Frenchman Street."

"No—no—please God, no!"

"He was standing close to a vehicle that exploded. We think it was murder, but we have to prove it."

"Who would murder—?"

"I'm sorry to have to be the one to tell you."

Mrs. Bergeron held a hand to her face, tears splashing down, her nose running. Peck handed her tissues.

"Why would—?" she whimpered.

"Mrs. Bergeron, why don't you let Peck explain it? We need to ask questions that will help us find out why. The questions may hurt, but we need to tie up loose ends."

"Where's Anthony?"

"Mr. Bergeron is at the city morgue, Mrs. Bergeron. You may come in on your own or Peck can bring you in, so you can identify him. I'm sorry you had to hear it this way."

Sobbing, Mrs. Bergeron handed the phone to Peck. Peck put it on speaker.

"We'll find out who did this, Mrs. Bergeron."

"Who would want to kill my Anthony? He had no enemies."

"We plan to answer those questions," Larry said.

Peck ended the call and offered her a hand to pull her up and in.

"Mrs. Bergeron?" Peck started.

"My name is Christie," she said.

"Christie, I know we were going to buy food and diapers, but you think we can go somewhere, sit and talk? You think, maybe?"

"The sitter brings Pull-Ups. We can talk, I guess."

Peck drove to the Ponchartrain Hotel, parked on the corner, and they went into the Silver Whistle Café.

"Can we talk without my having to relive it— please?" Christie asked.

"How you mean?"

"S'il vous plaît, ne me dites pas comment Anthony est mort. Je ne suis tout simplement pas prêt pour cela maintenant, s'il vous plait," Christie said. ("Please don't tell me how Anthony died. I'm just not ready for that now, please.")

"I promise. Can I ax you some questions?"

"Yes."

"Today when I went to your purdy shotgun on Magazine Street, the babies were alone. Little Bernadette, she told me nobody come two, maybe three days. Is that sweet girl right?"

"I don't know," Christie said. "Anthony should have been home, but now I just don't know."

"Can I ax where you were, Christie?"

"I don't know that, either. I was kidnapped."

"Hanh?"

"I put the kids to bed."

"When did you put them to bed, bébé?"

"It was the usual—seven o'clock."

"Was Anthony with you?"

"Anthony was at work—he works until ten. I told Bernadette I was going to make a shopping list, and I had to get diapers—we were out of diapers."

"What kind of work did Anthony do?"

"He played piano at a restaurant. They stop serving at ten and he comes home."

"Can I ax, why the—how you say—cupboards were bare, Christie? They were empty 'cept for the soup cans."

"Anthony brings dinners home from the restaurant for him and me. We grocery shop for cooked meals on payday—the first and the fifteenth. Anthony's pay is regular, mine is sporadic—when I can find work. The day I was kidnapped I had job interviews set up while he watched the babies."

"So, you come home after your job interviews, he goes to work and you tuck the kiddos in and then you go make a shopping list?"

"Yes."

"Then what?"

"I started to make the list but the doorbell rang."

"And you answered it?"

"That's when they grabbed me."

"Grabbed you?"

"They forced me out of the house."

"Who grabbed you, Christie?"

"I think two men—but they had masks."

"Can you remember what happened?"

"They took me to a van—it had lettering on it—and inside they blindfolded me with duct tape. They tied my wrists."

"Did they tell you what they were doing?"

"It was a computer voice."

"A computer? I don't understand."

"A computer talked to me."

"What, how you say, did this computer say?"

"It said, '*If you scream—make any sound, we will kill your children.*'"

"*Aye yi-yi,*" Peck whispered.

Peck's eyes winced as if his kidnapped childhood was flashing before his eyes. As if he could remember being chained under a porch and looking through the grates at a full moon and thinking the moon was his mamma—and begging her forgiveness if he had done something wrong.

"Are you okay?" Christie asked. "Have you heard anything I've said?"

"Christie, Anthony loved you, and he loved those babies—he was arrested with another man for smoking marijuana and taken to jail."

"No way."

"That's why he didn't come home."

"Anthony didn't smoke or do drugs. That can't be true."

"It is true, he was arrested."

"He was?"

"Ah *oui.*"

"When?"

Peck paused in thought. He interrupted the moment, stood up and pushed his chair in.

"Cher—those babies need their momma—they need their momma right now, this minute."

"But the lieutenant—" Christie started.

"Don't worry about the lieutenant. A few days is a lifetime to babies. A momma needs to be with her babies. Those babies need you right now. Shame on Peck for taking you away. Besides, your brain will work better after hugging those babies."

"Are you giving up?"

"Nah-nah, never."

"What about my Anthony?"

"You have you money, Christie? Food and things?"

"*Oui.*"

"You have a grocer who'll deliver?"

"*Oui.*"

"I'm taking you home, frien'—to those babies."

"You're giving up." Christie patted her tears with a napkin.

"I'm making a promise, Christie. I'm going to tell it way it is. It was my pickup that exploded. Your Anthony was standing beside it."

Christie stared at Peck glassy eyed.

"I promise I'll never give up until we know who did this and why, Mrs. Bergeron."

"They were trying to kill you, but Anthony was killed instead?"

"Ah *oui.*"

"Why did you tell me that?"

"You know *gris-gris*, bébé—?"

"I know *gris-gris.*"

"Nobody goes through two bad somethings like this without some serious *gris-gris.*"

"Two? I don't understand."

"Your being kidnapped and not told why and him dying—and he never smoked or did drugs."

"Are you thinking me getting taken and Anthony's dying are connected?"

"You think you can trust me, Christie?"

"It's hard for me to trust anyone, but because of Bernadette—I think I can trust you."

"I need some time to think. You need some time to remember. The best thinkin' I did in my life was hiding in a dark hole in a cypress tree—hiding from a man who hurt me and my mamma. That's when I did my best thinking, cher— alone in the dark for two days. I was nine."

"You need me to think and try to remember?"

"Dass for true, and best way to clear your head and remember—"

"—is to be with my babies?"

"Ah *oui*," Peck said. "Those babies need their momma—they need her hugs."

"And you need time to think," Christie said.

"I'm going to Baton Rouge to think and so tomorrow I see my reader. When I come back day after that, you and me we'll have us a lunch and I'll ax questions and I'll track who did this to you and to your Anthony. That okay, Christie?"

"Don't you want to—?"

"A momma's brain works better when momma knows the little ones are safe and all right. Two days, bébé, I'll be back and we go and talk. Maybe we go to Dookie Chase for gumbo. You let those babies look at momma's eyes and feel their momma's smiles and hugs."

"Bernadette was right," Christie said.

"How's that, cher?"

"She said you were a good man."

"So, it's okay I go to my reader—see you the next day?"

"What do I tell Bernadette about her daddy?"

"I lit three candles for her daddy this morning at Mass. Tell her that her daddy is making records—playing piano and he can't come home for a while."

Tears glistened in Christie's eyes.

"Who is your reader?" she asked.

"Her name is Audrey. I met her in Baton Rouge. I trust her."

"Do I have to go see Anthony?"

"Nah, nah, not until we're ready. Anthony would want you to wait. He'd want you to hug them babies. I'll call the lieutenant—I'll tell him three maybe two days and you'll go identify Anthony."

"Do me a favor?" Christie asked.

"Anything," Peck said.

"Turn a card for me—see what I should do now?"

"Ah *oui* bébé. I will. You do me a favor?"

"If I can."

"Get you a pen and write down everything you can remember from those days they had you. Don't worry about—how you say—paragraphs, cher—write words that will remind you what you're thinking. Everything you remember seeing, hearing—even thoughts you remember—write them down. We'll put this—how you say—puzzle together after I come back—"

"I'll do my best."

"—and hug them babies."

Peck drove Christie home and waited until she opened the shotgun house door. She put a smile on her face, best she could, and stepped in.

She waved at Peck and closed the door.

16.

PECK WAS DRIVING to Baton Rouge with a look in his eye that he had tracking on his mind. With the disciplines he learned prepping snoods and trotlines when he was six, he stared at the road ahead as if organizing his thoughts and memorizing a list of the people he needed. The first was Elizabeth in Baton Rouge. Best friends since Peck was seventeen. He pressed to call a contact on his phone.

"Peck, is that you?" Elizabeth asked.

"Ah *oui*."

"Bonjour."

"Where you at, bébé? Are you in Paris, a famous chef cooking for those important people?"

"Oh, I wish, *mon ami*. Still in Baton Rouge, I'm afraid. So much to organize, to get ready—so many things—passport, work visa, facetime interviews. Soon, hopefully, but I'm still here. Want to buy some furniture—ha ha?"

"I 'm working on a murder case. Somebody blew up my pickup. I need Audrey—I need a reading. "

"What?!"

"Ah *oui*."

"Are you all right? Were you hurt?"

"I'm all right."

"You said murder—who was murdered?"

"Not now, cher—let me tell you later."

"Where are you now?"

"I'll be in Baton Rouge in an hour or so."

"Tu a besoin de plus qu'une lecture, Peck. Tu a besoin de moi," Elizabeth said. *(*"You need more than a reading, Peck. You need me."*)*

"Bébé, I got so much to go through in my head."

"I can only imagine."

"You and me we get in the tub like we used to?"

"When do you want to see Audrey?"

"Tomorrow morning?"

"Tonight, I cook or we go out. You choose, Peck."

"Can you get the French bistro to—how you say—deliver something so we can be together and talk?" Peck asked.

"*Absolument!*" Elizabeth said.

"See you soon, cher."

"I'll shave my legs," Elizabeth quipped.

Peck grinned, ended the call and touched the phone contact for Aurelie, his friend at the cell phone store on Canal Street.

Aurelie answered.

"I love when you call me."

"You do? Why's that, cher?"

"I get to talk like I did when I was a child in Church Point with my grandparents—my *Momo* and *Pépére*."

"I'm learning better, reading books," Peck said.

"Don't ever change, Peck."

"I'm just me—purdy much."

"Want to dance Dixieland, bébé?" Aurelie asked.

"If you promise to slow dance, I promise to call you when I get back."

"Back, Peck? Where y'at?"

"On my way to Baton Rouge. Seeing my reader."

"You want some more phones, Peck?"

"I need to ax if you can do something, bébé."

"Are these secret things you going to ask me about, maybe?"

"You okay with that?"

"Ask and we'll see."

"And keep secret?"

"Of course."

"There's a man named Anthony Bergeron, cher. He lives on Magazine Street. His wife is Christie."

"Okay so far."

"I need to see if you can find their phone numbers."

"I can probably do that."

"I need to find out who they called or who called them for the past six days, cher."

"Oh, now—this may be—" Aurelie started.

"He's been murdered and his lady was kidnapped for three days."

"I know how to do it."

"So, you'll do it for me, bébé?"

"Wait just a minute."

Peck kept his eyes on the road seeing mileage signs for Baton Rouge.

"Okay, I'm outside now," Aurelie said.

"Where you can talk better?"

"Ah *oui*—Peck I'll see what I can do. Can we meet at your place or at my apartment? I'll feel more comfortable not talking about this while I'm at work. You understand?"

"This help can maybe solve a murder. He was a daddy and they had a little baby and a ten-year-old girl. It's so sad."

"You still have the prepaid phones, Peck?"

"Ah *oui*. I do. It's at our shotgun. I have one left."

"Use it from now on when we talk about this."

"Okay."

"Will you really take me dancing?"

"I guarontee, cher."

"But you have a girlfriend."

"Nah nah—not so sure about that. Least for now."

"I'll get a pretty dress."

"Later, cher," Peck said, ending the call.

Peck pressed Larry's contact number.

"Talk to me," Larry said.

"This is a dark bayou, Larry. Lots of it covered with pond cypress and blackgum plants."

"Making headway, son?"

"I'm seeing the way—but I need to see more."

"Explain."

"We focusing on a house on Magazine Street—already have lots from that. But it's a big mistake to just look at what we think we want. We have to study what else was going on that would make a man in a tuxedo try to steal a truck."

"Tell me what you need, son."

"Larry, something bad happened to that man Anthony—same time something bad happened to his lady, and she didn't know he disappeared. Something ain't right, Larry. Too—how you say—coincidental."

"And—?" Larry asked.

"From what I know so far it looks like maybe it was well-organized. If it was well-organized, maybe it's been going on and we just haven't seen it before. Maybe this was their mistake in our favor."

"I love your brain, Peck."

17.

ELIZABETH OPENED THE DOOR wearing nothing but a *toque* (chef hat). Arms outstretched, she let Peck walk to her, folding around him like French pastry, snuggling her nose to his neck.

"*Je veux te tenir pour toujours*," Elizabeth said. ("I want to hold you forever.")

"*Si nous ne faisons pas d'anglais, cher, Peck ne parlera pas mieux et la Français me rappellera simplement Paris et je ne vous reverrai jamais*." ("If we don't do English, cher, Peck won't talk better and the French will just remind me of Paris and my never seeing you again.")

With a devilish look in her eye Elizabeth nudged Peck back against the door, closing it behind him. She grabbed the bottom of his T-shirt and tugged it up, over his head and off. She knelt on the floor, unbuckled his belt and unzipped his jeans.

"I miss your beautiful long black hair, *cher*—it frames those green eyes oh so like a fine painting—dass for true," Peck said.

Elizabeth smiled and pulled his jeans down deliberately, slowly never taking her eyes from his.

"I still have my hair, Peck—an important chef has to tuck hair under the toque."

Peck stepped out of his jeans.

As Elizabeth reached up to tug his briefs down and off, Peck lifted the toque from her head—her black hair dropping down to her shoulders.

"You are so beautiful, cher. You still—how you say—got it."

Pulling his briefs down Elizabeth watched his William and its growing swagger. She smiled. "As do you, *mon ami*."

She stood and took Peck's hand and led him to a bathtub filled with sudsy bubbles and warmth. They crawled in as if it were their private treehouse—Peck sat between her legs, his back to her. Elizabeth scrubbed his back with the sponge … He rambled on about how they met when he was seventeen and how he followed her home, walking backward and barefoot, talking to her all the way on the hot 103-degree day. Of how he would walk eleven miles from Carencro to the Cajun chicken restaurant where she was sous chef. How they made love for the first time but thought of themselves as best friends forever more than lovers. They would watch the morning moons and see in them the crepes Elizabeth would make for him and in the morning's red sky, the jams she would decorate them with.

Bath towels wrapped and knotted around their waists, they let the Bistro's young delivery boy cop glance as he set the coffee table up with flatware and napkins so they could sit on the floor, dine—and talk.

"I'm lucky to be alive, cher," Peck said.

"Only tell me when you're ready, Peck. I don't want you to relive it, but I want to hear the whole story. Telling it will help you heal."

Peck retold the evening on Frenchman Street—the hail, the explosions, how Sasha was injured. He spoke with sadness about the mystery man killed in the fiery blaze and how he found the man's children helpless and hungry. He told of the promise he made to the man's widow that he would exact a toll on whoever made this happen.

"Audrey's reading will bring light on things for you, Peck. Maybe the cards will show you a path."

They shared pâté on butter knives, feeding each other between the punctuations of thoughts and sentences. Elizabeth touched varieties of olives and strawberries into honey and held them out for Peck's mouth—teasing him with them and kissing honey from his lips.

Elizabeth went to the bedroom first and laid on the bed. When Peck walked in Elizabeth sat up, unknotted his towel, and dropped it to the floor. Sitting on the side of the bed, she was hinting that she was available. She had him lay on his stomach, then stood, dropped her towel to the floor, turned the bedside lamp off and straddled his buttocks in the dark, scratching his back—gently from his neck to the base of his spine until he fell asleep. She watched him in the glow of the streetlamps outside. She smiled as if she was thinking of memories they shared for a decade, growing up together. Elizabeth in her mid-twenties was Peck's first lover. He was seventeen. She was living with an oil rig worker at the time but not married. Peck was her first true love. This night her beautiful green eyes watched him as if she was counting the freckles on his back—thinking of them as stars in the sky— memories.

She rested on his back and fell asleep.

18.

WHEN SHE AWOKE, Elizabeth was straddling Peck, crouched on his waist—her face nestled his neck.

Her yawn awakened him.

"What time do I see Audrey?" he grunted.

"At ten."

"Ah, okay."

Elizabeth yawned again.

"What would you like for breakfast, Peck?"

"You've been packing, cher. What you have?"

"Coddled eggs, crepes and jam, boudin sausages."

"*Parfait*," Peck mused. ("Perfect.")

Elizabeth lifted her head, guffawed, and sat up on his buttocks.

"*Parfait? Parfait*?" she barked. "You want it all?"

She reached behind, between his legs and clutched his jewels.

"Mr. sleepy man with personal service from the newest chef in Baton Rouge—if you get everything, what's in it for the chef, eh?"

"You mean what's in it for the best chef in Paris?" Peck asked.

Elizabeth grinned with a look of surprise and loosened her grip on the *boys*.

"Oh my, *merci*," she said.

"What's in it for the best chef in the world, cher?"

Elizabeth climbed off and stood next to the bed, as if she was about to tear up with pride. Peck turned on his side looked at her green eyes. He slid a hand between her legs and moved it on a warm inner thigh up near her love.

"Maybe we think of something," he mused.

Elizabeth smiled a bathtub treehouse-like smile.

"Let me go see Audrey," Peck said. "I'll see what she says, what I should do. Then we'll do lunch ... *au lit peut-être?*" (*...in bed maybe?"*)

Elizabeth squeezed her thighs against his hand.

"So, are you turning me down?" Peck asked.

Elizabeth answered by gripping his wrist and gently pulling it to her love island with a wry smile.

"I'm so not turning you down, *mon ami. Ce sera mon plaisir,*" she whispered. ("It'll be my pleasure.")

"*Le mien aussi, cher,*" Peck said. ("*Mine too.*")

"I have a breakfast to make for a prince among men—e*xcusez-moi, s'il vous plaît?*"

While Peck and Elizabeth were sharing breakfast in Baton Rouge and getting ready for his Tarot reading with Audrey, Larry was in his bedroom across Lake Ponchartrain in Covington reaching for his phone.

"Talk to me," Larry said.

"Chris here, Lieutenant."

"My favorite coroner. It's early Chris, even for you—talk to me."

"Lieutenant, you said you wanted first look on any robberies that came up, right?"

"I do, Chris—Officer Downs informed me of a jewelry store robbery that took place yesterday."

"I have another one, Lieutenant. This one is a burglary attempt, sir. Happened this morning."

"It's not even ten, Chris—stores aren't open. Was it a break in?"

"Happened around 3:00 a.m., Lieutenant. Just discovered. Officer Downs called me. Don't know why he would call me first and not dispatch."

"Because you're the man, Chris. No one hears any more—everybody listens but they don't hear. Thanks for the call, my friend."

"Lieutenant, would your interest—you know, your request about first looks at robberies—would your interest also include first looks at burglaries?"

"It would."

"Then I have a body you should look at."

"At the morgue?"

"No."

"Where?"

"At the scene."

"Talk to me."

"D&A Jewelers—on Hampson, Lieutenant. I think the door lock was picked—no other signs of entry."

"I think I bought a desk lamp there, Chris."

"You could have, Lieutenant. It's Diamonds and Antiques—the D&A."

"Pricey."

"It's top of the line, sir—we have a body doing the backstroke in a pool of blood on a priceless imported rug."

"Are you in New Orleans, Lieutenant?"

"I'm in Covington, Chris—having some work done on my house."

"Oh, I thought maybe you were at Counselor Tarleton's house in the district."

"It's a long drive in—heavy traffic. Can you give me a few hours?"

"If I do, Lieutenant, I'm going to need you to cover my ass on this one."

"How so?"

"With the chief, think you can do that?"

"What's to cover?"

"I haven't called Forensics yet—I wanted you to see the scene first. If I stall that call a couple of hours, it could mean my head."

"You're covered, my friend."

"Thank you, Lieutenant."

"Don't put up crime tape, Chris—have the owner put the *closed* sign, *out to lunch* sign—something—on the front door and keep it locked. Pull the shade."

"Roger that, Lieutenant."

"I'll see you soon, Chris."

19.

WHILE LARRY WAS GETTING READY to drive the causeway from Covington to New Orleans, Peck was enjoying a warm morning walk in Baton Rouge. Long strolls stirred Peck's memory cells, helping him think. He walked to Audrey's for his tarot reading, taking in the sights and sounds. When he got to Audrey's door, Audrey was waiting for him, standing in the window, sipping tea. He pulled the door open. Audrey held her arms out for a hug.

"Peck, you are such an anomaly for me."

"Ha! I'll have to look that one up—anomaly, you say?"

"I'll make it easy for you, Peck. I am happy to see you—I admire you—but it's getting that it's almost sad to see you, because you come when someone is being hurt in New Orleans."

"It's always good to see you," Peck said.

This time Audrey locked the door and took Peck into the kitchen, poured him a tea and sat him at the porcelain kitchen table. There was a tarot deck sitting on the table.

"Peck, I don't want to cloud this reading, but later I would like to know if you've heard anything from that little girl you saved from the slaver."

"Telling you about it won't cloud anything, Miss Audrey. Chloe is living in Oklahoma now with Lauren and her family. Small farm with horses and goats and a school bus that comes by. They're adopting her, so she'll have their name. Lauren is a full nurse now, and is Chloe's big sister. Lauren agreed with me that the best thing for Chloe to do is like what Lieutenant Larry in New Orleans told me to do— stop looking back at my past. I'm thinking it's best they don't look back or keep in touch. Just move on."

"Peck, it's an honor just to know you."

"Nah-nah, cher—you're the one to honor. You found me my whole life introducing me to Dr. Price and the—how you say—hypnosis and that's when I found my mamma. I'll never forgot that, Audrey. You maybe saved my life doing that."

Audrey reached across the table and took Peck's hands into hers.

"You've come all this way, again, Boudreaux. Tell me the whole story. Tell me everything. We have plenty of tea and time."

"It started Sunday, Audrey. There was a hail storm in New Orleans Sunday and Sunday night is when I go to work—I clean Sasha's real-estate offices in the Garden District and then I drive over to Carrolton Avenue and clean Lily Cup's law offices. I do them on Sunday night. I started my pickup while I was inside Charlie's—you know—the Blue Note. I went outside in the ice and I saw somebody standing behind my pickup like they was looking in it. Sasha came outside to give me my phone—I forgot and left it inside—and then *Boom!* My pickup blew up and we flew into the bushes. Sasha got pretty tore up."

"My heavens," Audrey said.

"Miss Audrey, the reason I'm here today is that the man who was standing by my pickup is dead, and he was a father and a good husband."

"Peck, I know you well enough to know you see everything. From your early days just surviving in the hidden bayous and swamps, you've developed instincts for observation of a wild animal."

"Ah *oui.*"

"Peck are you here to get a reading about what's in store for this man's family?"

"Partly, Miss Audrey. I'm trying to solve how it happened and why it happened. And there's more."

"Tell me when you can."

"The man who got killed—his wife and mother of two babies was kidnapped about the same time."

Audrey blessed herself with the sign of the cross.

"You're helping your lieutenant friend investigate this, am I right, Peck?"

"Ah *oui*."

"Is the mother still kidnapped?"

"Nah-nah, she's at home again, I talked to her. I'll see her tomorrow after the reading."

"I see."

"She ax me to pull a card for her too. She's so scared with no husband and daddy to them babies now."

"What's the mother's name?"

"Christie."

Audrey had an assortment of different styled tarot card decks. She held out a tray for Peck to choose the deck they would read from.

"Today we'll pull three cards, Peck. One we'll pull for Christie. One we'll pull for you. The top card will be for me—it'll give me a feel of where things stand."

"You think only two—one for me and one for Christie, Miss Audrey?"

"You have a wonderful mind, Peck. You only need a window or two to look through. I can read what I see, but you will hear me and maybe it will open windows in that beautiful mind of yours."

"Thank you, cher."

"Peck, take the deck out of its pack."

Peck obliged.

"Lay the deck on the table."

Peck obliged.

"To bring your energy, Peck, knock on the deck several times."

Peck counted three knocks on the deck with his knuckles.

"Cut the deck into three piles."

Peck cut the deck.

"Now put the piles together and shuffle."

Peck was thorough in shuffling. He set the cards in the middle of the table.

"I'm lifting the top card," Audrey said. She lifted the top card and placed it face down in front of her.

"Please fan the deck out, Peck, and select two cards."

Peck floated his palm back and forth over the fan of tarot cards. He pointed at one and pushed it out. He then pointed at a second one and pushed that out as well.

"These, Miss Audrey. This one for Christie and this other one for me."

Audrey turned her card first.

"The Devil card, Peck. Possibly the worst card there is. We are being told that the situation is broader than the one incident of the man being killed. Influences and forces beyond this family's control are restricting them, thus restricting you in your search for the truth."

"That's bad for me, then," Peck said.

"Not totally Peck. The Devil card tries to victimize you by leaving the illusion that you are powerless and victimized. It's an illusion, Peck. Don't give in to it. You are in control, should you choose."

"Ah *oui*. I choose, dass for true."

"Peck, please turn your card."

Peck turned his card. It was the Eight of Cups.

This is so telling, Peck. I do believe you will benefit from this reading."

"Thank you, Miss Audrey."

"The Eight of Cups means abandonment, Peck. The mother was kidnapped to appear she was walking away from her family and responsibilities. The father was led to believe she was gone and would only come back if he was ready to make a sacrifice."

"To steal something? Like my pickup?"

"It could have been any demand, Peck. Yes. It could have been stealing your pickup."

"So you think her kidnap and his stealing is connected, Miss Audrey?"

"Peck, turn Christie's card, please."

Peck turned the Eight of Swords. Audrey gasped.

"What is it, Miss Audrey? What's wrong?"

Audrey blessed herself with a sign of the cross.

"You can see the woman, trapped like a slave with a ball and chain, Peck?"

"Ah *oui*."

"This card, the Eight of Swords means two things for you, Peck."

"Okay, good."

"It means feeling trapped, confined, backed into a corner, having hands tied."

"They taped her hands, Miss Audrey. They taped her eyes."

"They use fear, terror, and psychological issues."

"Miss Audrey—they left the kids behind, alone."

"A moment of silence, please, Peck."

Audrey lowered her head in thought.

She then sat up straight.

"Is our Christie a strong woman, Peck?"

"She is so strong. I can tell it by knowing a little about her, but I can tell it by knowing her little babies."

"That is so good to hear. If she can keep herself from thinking negative thoughts that paralyze us—she can remove the blindfold, walk away and help you with the answers you need to solve the case."

"Miss Audrey, you said the Eight of Swords means two things. What's the other thing?"

"The second thing is this, Peck. This is saying Christie is only one of many who are being victimized in this same way."

"*Aye-yi-yi*," Peck said.

"My thoughts too, Peck."

"So I have to find the center—how you say—the core of who's doing this."

"Exactly."

"And you think her being kidnapped and his stealing my pickup are linked, right, Miss Audrey?"

"It's in the cards, Peck. It's all in the cards."

"*Aye yi-yi*," Peck whispered.

"Now it's up to you, Peck."

20.

AS PECK WALKED BACK to Elizabeth's apartment in Baton Rouge, he called Larry in New Orleans.

"Talk to me, son."

"Larry, I have a feeling we need to go back some days and see what robberies and things happened. And we need to go forward and watch every day."

"What's on your mind, Peck?"

"My tarot reading with Miss Audrey up here in Baton Rouge maybe—how you say—opened my eyes, Larry. I need to pirogue look at the swamp ... see where crawfish snakes are nesting ... where the snappers are gettin' sun warmed. I got to see where the mashwarohn roll their fat bellies at the top by the lily pads and dive to the bottom to feed."

"You're talking metaphors, right son?"

"Pretty sure, Larry. Ah *oui*."

"Talk to me straight."

"Larry, I need to see every burglary that happened in New Orleans back ten days and I want to see anything that happens for the next week or so."

"Chris called me in on another jewelry store, this time a burglary—happened in the night, Peck. I'm on my way there now. I'll get you the details."

"Officer Downs called me on that one, Larry. You sent me there. I already checked it out. The one on Maple Street, right?"

"The Maple Street job is old news, Peck. This one is on Hampson. Middle of the night burglary. Different store, different MO. A body found."

"*Aye yi-yi*. I'll need to see if they tie together, Larry."

"I get it. You're looking for the chum, you're looking for the link—the lady gone missing and her husband's stealing."

"Ah *oui*. The cards say ever'thing I'm seeing could be connected—and if they're all connected—there might could be something bigger going on, Larry."

"Where do you want them—the papers?"

"I can get them from you at Lily Cup's when I come back."

"Which will be when?"

"Leaving here soon."

"I'll be in touch with you on the past ones. I'll have Officer Downs call you with the day-to-day ones," Larry said.

"Thanks, frien'."

"Good luck tracking, son."

"One more thing, Larry."

"Okay."

"That room we talked in over at the precinct?"

"The interrogation room?"

"Ah *oui*, that's it. Larry can I use it to talk to the dead man's lady, please? I could use the marker board to make notes when she remembers things."

"Be our guest, Peck. I'll tell the station desk to reserve it. You need anything else, pin boards, markers, maps—just ask the front desk sergeant on duty."

"Thanks, Larry. See you soon."

Peck unlocked Elizabeth's door and walked in to find Elizabeth on a FaceTime interview with a restaurant owner in Paris. He went to the kitchen, found a notepad and scratched a message and held it out for her to read.

"Let me go solve this thing in New Orleans—then I come back and we celebrate Paris? Oui?"

He handed it to her to read. She looked at him and winked that she understood.

As Peck left Elizabeth's apartment to drive back to New Orleans, Larry was on Hampson Street, stepping inside the D & A store and meeting the coroner. He saw the body for the first time.

"It's a woman, Chris—you never said it was a woman."

"Dead's dead, Lieutenant. Didn't think it was relevant—the sex of the deceased."

"That's a lot of blood, Chris."

"Head wounds bleed extensively, Lieutenant."

"Cause of death?"

"Lieutenant, our burglar suspect here was shot one time in the head. It was a .38 revolver. The gun's on a counter in the back room. My guess is that gun did it. Haven't examined her closely. With all the blood in her hair, I'm not certain where the bullet entered."

"I know Forensics hasn't been here, but what's your trusted nose for evidence have to say, Chris?"

"Lieutenant, I smelled the gun—it was on the floor by the stairs. It's definitely the weapon used. A .38 special. I looked in its cylinder. Each chamber had a spent casing in it. So six shots were fired. The one that hit her in the head fatally dropping her—instantly, I would imagine. I'll know more with an autopsy."

Larry moved his flashlight about the store interior. He could see a missing store window over the door and two bullet holes in another window.

"Of the six shots, one hit the lady, two went into the front wall, and two through the front store window. Single small holes likely means the store windows are bulletproof. Then there's the small stained glass window pane up over the door—my guess is a bullet shattered it—and we'll likely find it in one of the phone poles on the sidewalk."

"Six rounds, one hit. An amateur," Larry said.

"How are you so sure, Lieutenant?"

"Chris, a cop or security guard could take someone down with one, maybe two shots. But he'd never waste six shots and be defenseless without ammo in his gun. And a cop would never aim for the head, especially inside. They'd go for the heart—to minimize the risk of missing the body altogether."

"That sounds right to me. So this is how I think it went down, Lieutenant. It so happens the daughter of the store owner was asleep upstairs when she heard glass breaking down here around—best guess—3:45 this morning. She crept down the stairs with a revolver her father trained her to use. She pointed the gun and asked who was there. She asked twice, got no response, heard a noise, and she emptied the gun, all six rounds. She said she was certain she had scared them off, so she went upstairs and called 911."

"So, according to the shooter she was not trying to hit the burglar, just trying to scare her?"

"Looks that way, Lieutenant. Officer Downs showed up, looked in the window with his flashlight, saw bullet holes and the body and called me."

"Well," Larry started. "That explains five misses and one in the head. But look at the body, Chris. That's a fashionable dress on the corpse. She certainly doesn't look like a cat burglar working in the dark. I wonder what possessed the shooter to—"

"She's blind, Lieutenant."

"This victim is blind, Chris?"

"No, our shooter is blind, sir."

"The girl upstairs? The one who fired—?"

"Yes, sir. She's nineteen, Lieutenant, and totally blind since birth."

"Blind as in—?"

"Zero vision, sir. Her name is Patricia. She came to visit her dad from her mother's home in Jackson. Her dad left her alone. The store was to be closed three days. She came to keep the parrot company as a favor to her dad. She told me he's on a cruise with the store manager. Thinks he's going to propose to her on the cruise."

"Sounds like you've pretty well wrapped it up, Chris. The shooter was protecting her life and her father's property. Same circumstances, you and I would have probably done the same. Open and shut."

"I pretty much agree, Lieutenant—with one exception."

"Yeah?"

"It's not open and shut."

"Talk to me."

"There was a ball peen hammer on the floor partially hidden by the dead body. Chris picked it up with a handkerchief. Lieutenant, step around and take a look from that angle at the glass counter that's been broken."

Larry stepped around to the back side of the counter with the watches in it.

"Chris, the counter is padlocked and the glass was hit with that hammer—broken here with one blow. Over there, about, say four feet away, with another blow. A simple smash and grab. Our burglar smashes the glass on this watch display case, the blind girl upstairs hears the noise and comes down the stairs. Our burglar smashes the second display glass, and the blind girl shoots at the sound—and the burglar gets dropped before she has a chance to grab. The watches are still in the cabinet, Chris. You see it different?"

"Lieutenant, I took pictures you should look at."

Chris held his iPhone up for Larry to see.

"I took these pictures earlier, Lieutenant. There was a morning sun reflecting from some of the antiques."

"What am I looking at, Chris?"

"Pictures of the broken piece of glass, Lieutenant. If you look at different pieces of the glass in these pictures it looks like there's writing on it. What do you make of it?"

"It looks like a circle, Chris. Someone drew a circle on the glass—"

"I see it."

"And can you see the small *x* inside the circle, Lieutenant?"

"Faintly, but, yes, I can see it," Larry said.

"Now look at the same pieces of glass in the case, Lieutenant."

"I can't see it on any of the glass, Chris. The circle and the *x* don't show up. Have they been wiped? Help me out here, what's on your mind?"

Chris handed Larry his sunglasses.

"Lieutenant, I had to wear my prescription sunglasses today. When I saw the writing on the glass but not with the naked eye, I experimented and used my glasses as a filter to take the pictures through these. I was wearing them when I came in. My regular glasses are being repaired—waiting for me at the optometrist but I've been here since 4:30 this morning."

Chris removed his sunglasses and handed them to Larry.

"Put these on and try them, Lieutenant.

Larry put Chris's sunglasses on.

"Now, look at the counter glass again, Lieutenant."

"I'll be damned," Larry said. "I can see it clear as a bell."

"Invisible ink, Lieutenant. On that other piece of broken glass, same circle and an *x*."

"Talk to me, Chris."

"I think it's an inside job, Lieutenant."

"Let's back up, Chris—let's not get ahead of ourselves. A woman in her thirties breaks in—picks a lock— or however, but she breaks in to burglarize with sunglasses in the dark. Doesn't make sense."

"The lights were on, Lieutenant."

"They were?"

"Yes, sir."

"So, sunglasses would work for reading the invisible ink—"

"Yes."

"And the blind girl wouldn't know the lights were on."

"That's right, Lieutenant."

"And she wouldn't have turned them on, because she's blind."

"Yes, Lieutenant."

"Does our body have a purse, Larry?"

"It's on her shoulder, Lieutenant."

"Open it. Check for sunglasses."

"Here they are, Lieutenant. And the pocketbook wasn't snapped closed."

"Any ID?"

"Lieutenant, these are men's sunglasses. Why would she have men's sunglasses?"

"An accomplice? Have Forensics check them for prints."

"Yes sir."

"Her name, Chris?"

"Her name is Marilyn Knotts."

"What is that outfit she's wearing, Chris? Is it a house dress?"

"It's like a painter's smock, Lieutenant. One of our forensic ladies wears one—black like this one. They're a trendy Italian thing. Dressy and casual. Deep pockets."

"I can't see her hands, Chris."

"May I turn the body, Lieutenant?"

"Let's do it."

They rolled the corpse onto its back.

"*Rigor* is setting in," Larry said.

"Both hands in her pockets Lieutenant."

"Let's see what they're hiding, Chris. If you can move them."

Chris pulled one hand out of a pocket. It was clutching a Rolex watch. The hand in the other pocket was also clutching a Rolex.

"Interesting," Larry said. "That shoots my smash and grab scenario."

"How so, Lieutenant?"

"You smash and grab, you grab a lot. Our Marilyn Knotts here picked a couple of watches—one in each hand."

"The x, Lieutenant."

"Precisely. The invisible ink circle for the area in the display. The invisible ink x for the exact watch—in this case the two watches."

"Look, Lieutenant. One is a man's Rolex—the other is a woman's Rolex."

"Code on back, Chris—I'm thinking they're worth in the range of fifty thousand each."

"What now, Lieutenant? Can I call in Forensics?"

"Give me just a second, Chris."

Larry walked to the back stair that led up to the apartment above. He shouted up.

"Patricia?"

A parrot squawked above.

"Patricia?"

The door at the top of the stairs opened, Patricia was in a Turkish bathrobe, wearing blacked out glasses.

"Yes? What is it?" Patricia asked.

"Patricia, I'm Lieutenant Miller with the police. I'm investigating the burglary."

"Thank you, Lieutenant. It was frightening," Patricia said. "Did they take anything?"

"No ma'am…doesn't appear so."

"Thank God I scared them off."

"Patricia, do you know a Marilyn Knotts?"

"Yes, sir."

"You know Marilyn Knotts?

"Marilyn manages Daddy's store. Do you need her?"

"Ahh—no ma'am, thank you."

"Marilyn is on a cruise with my dad. They have no signal. Should I ask her to call you when they get back?"

"No, Patricia. I'm just taking notes."

"Thank you."

"Patricia, what is your daddy's name?"

"Same as mine, Melancon—spelled as it sounds."

"Patricia, there will be people in and out for a while today, do you need food sent up or anything?"

"No, I'll be fine. I'm listening to audio books, waiting for my dad and Marilyn to come back. They left me everything I need."

"Have a good day, Patricia,"

Larry walked over to Chris.

"I think she thinks she scared a burglar off, Chris."

"I have a cousin who is blind, Lieutenant. He has a way of sensing things. I'm thinking our blind girl upstairs heard sounds that shouldn't be in the store at three in the morning, came down, shot without aiming to scare them away. I think she felt she was doing the right thing—giving the intruder the opportunity to speak up. Our Marilyn here very likely laughed, knowing Patricia is blind and continued her burglary. Patricia heard another crash but this time shot at the sound, protecting herself and her daddy's livelihood the way her dad taught her."

"Chris, keep Marilyn's name out of the news until the store owner comes back. We'll let him deal with his daughter."

"This Marilyn was supposed to be on a cruise with him, Lieutenant? Is that what I heard?"

"It is. Any keys in her purse, Chris?"

"Yes, sir—here they are."

Larry took the keys. One of them unlocked the padlock on the watch display case. Chris looked in awe.

"Our Marilyn here had the keys all along, but broke the glass," Larry said.

"What do you make of it, sir?"
"I think we need Peck," Larry said.

21.

DRIVING TO NEW ORLEANS, Peck slowed to search his phone for the number of his friend Aurelie at the phone store on Canal Street. She requested that if they were talking about the business of her searching personal phone records of people, he use a prepaid phone for those calls so it couldn't be traced. As she requested, he touched the number into his prepaid phone and pressed *call*.

"Who's calling please?"

"Aurelie, this is Peck. I'm using the prepaid like you ax."

"Hi."

"Hello, bébé—how you are?"

"Peck, give me a minute to step outside, please?"

"Ah *oui*. I understand."

Passing a group of Cypress stumps in a bayou, Peck watched a blue heron dive into the water.

"Okay I can talk now," Aurelie said.

"Bébé, I just saw a heron dive into the bayou—so beautiful."

"*La nature me manque, vivre ici dans la ville, Peck. Un jour, peut-être que vous irez avec moi à Church Point et rencontrerez mes grands parents—mon Momo et Pépére.*" ("I miss nature—living here in the city, Peck. Someday maybe you'll go with me to Church Point and meet my grandparents—my Momo and Pépére.")

"Maybe I can do that."

"Good fishing in Church Point, I promise."

"We'll plan a trip for sure. Did you have any luck with phone calls Mr. or Mrs. Bergeron made or received?" Peck asked.

"I did. They have two phones. I have a printout of the calls they made and received for six days."

"Oh, cher, you're the best, dass for true."

"When can we meet?" Aurelie asked.

"I have to call some people, Aurelie. I have to see if I need to meet with them this morning—then I'll know when we can meet. Can I call you back?"

"Are we going to meet at your place or my apartment, Peck? I work until six."

"You decide," Peck said.

"You like jambalaya?"

"My mouth is watering already, bébé."

"My apartment. I'll cook."

"*Au revoir.*"

Peck clicked off and touched *Larry* on his iPhone.

"Talk to me."

"Larry, I'm back."

"Learn anything from your teller, Peck?"

"Miss Audrey is not a teller, Larry. She's a reader."

"Oh, sorry."

"I learned so much. Eight of Cups is a big one, I'll say," Peck said.

"What's it mean?" Larry asked.

"It means abandonment, Larry—they take everything away from them and make them do anything."

"What's the plan?"

"First, I'm going to see Christie Bergeron, take her to your station and ax some things—see what she remembers. Then I'm checking out some things I can't tell you about."

"Keeping a fishing hole to yourself, are you son?"

"Let's just say by not telling you some things, I'm keeping you out of trouble."

"You're the man, Peck. Can you give me an hour or two right now?"

"How you mean?"

"Can you meet me now?"

"I can. Where?"

"City morgue."

"Larry, let me stop by our shotgun to say hello to ol' Gabe first, and then I'll be on my way, okay? I ain't seen him since all this happened."

"Take your time, son. Say *hey* to my brother," Larry said. "See you at the morgue when you get there."

The call ended. Peck's phone rang. He saw it was Elizabeth.

"How you are, cher?" he asked.

"*Est-ce M. Boudreaux Clemont Finch, le célèbre détective privé à qui je parle?*" Elizabeth asked. ("Is this Mr. Boudreaux Clemont Finch, the famous private detective to whom I am speaking?")

"It is, j*eune fille*." (young lady.)

"You make me young, you gorgeous man."

"You sound happy, *mon cher*. Did your—how you say—interview with that important-sounding man go well?"

"*Monsieur*, you happen to be speaking with a head chef of a new bistro opening up on the Left Bank in Paris. They want to have the flair and tastes of New Orleans. They will have jazz."

"I am oh so proud of you bébé, congratulations. When do you leave?"

"In six weeks."

"Ah, so I will get to see you before you go."

"Peck—promise me you will solve that murder and then come here before I leave and we'll make love like the first time."

"Ah *oui*—but I was seventeen then, cher and you had to do most everything to teach me."

"*Exactement*," Elizabeth said.

"You are such a naughty—but I'm pulling into where I have a meeting. Congratulations, chef—love you my frien' and I'll see you soon."

Peck clicked off.

22.

PECK WALKED IN through the side kitchen door as Gabe came from his room. Gabe embraced him. It was the first time he'd seen his friend since the explosion.

"My brother," Gabe said.

"Ol' man, I'm sorry I haven't been in touch. I've been busy with things."

"My brother," Gabe said. "On my eighteenth birthday, I left home, walked into a recruiting station and joined the army. I didn't wait for my draft notice. I volunteered, joined, and stayed for thirty years. I trained in Kentucky, New Jersey, Texas. I've danced to jazz, some good some bad, from Harlem to Honolulu, from North Dakota to New Orleans—I fought and got shot at in Korea, Vietnam, and stood guard at the race riots in Detroit and Philadelphia. The first thing the army taught every recruit was to not ask questions. The second was to never question authority."

Peck kissed him on the cheek and stepped back, reaching for the coffee urn.

"My frien', I need me some chicory to hear where this story is going."

Gabe howled.

Peck filled Gabe's mug.

"Thirty years in the army, son. It told me you've been on a mission. I knew to be calm and stay low until you came home. I don't know what's going on—it's not for me to know. All I know is when brother Larry gave me a wink at Charlie's Blue Note the night your pickup exploded, I knew you weren't hurt. I knew Sasha was safe—and I knew God would bring you home one day."

"It's a mess out there, I'll say," Peck said.

"Times are changing, son, people's values are changing. It's not pretty."

"Gabe, why is it that birds like the heron I saw the other day seem to hunt smarter every time I see them? Gators get smarter too. I've seen a gator come at a cypress root from four different directions—testing. Crawfish snakes, frogs, even the mashwarohn—they'll send a young one down like to count crawfish or shrimp on the bottom before they roll and dive to feed. Why is it animals get smarter and us humans—we don't get any smarter. We get more ignorant ever day? Ain't we supposed to be the smartest animal, Gabe?"

"We're the dumbest animal, son. And we only use ten percent of our brains. Our momma's give us the teat for as long as we're lazy enough to take it. Our daddies don't teach us anything we can use to survive on. They only complain about their lot in life, and what others have—no matter what they do. It's all a mess, son. Today it's about me, me, me."

"You remember that day, Gabe? In Carencro?"

"At the hospice?"

"Ah *oui*," Peck said.

"You were baiting your snoods, Peck—getting ready to cast your trotline. You stuck a treble-hook in your hand, didn't bat an eye and walked over to me sitting there on the hospice's bench waiting to die and held up your bloody hand and handed me some needle-nose pliers to take the hooks out of your hand. Like it was yesterday, son."

"We run away from that hospice and Carencro, Gabe, and we went the wrong way and wound up here in New Orleans, in an alley off Frenchman Street—between an old strip bar and the fortune teller, massage lady—dancing jazz with purdy women at Charlie's Blue Note."

"What a night. My brother. Oh, what a night."

"Gabe, will I ever have fun again, frien'?"

"Let me teach you a trick, son."

"What's that, Gabe?"

"In the army, at night—you get in your billet."

"Billet, Gabe?"

"Your billet is where your cot is—where you sleep."

"Ah *oui*, okay."

"You're in your billet and a bugler plays taps. Taps is a soft, restful, pleasant, nostalgic sound. He plays it to remind you it's time to put the day out of your head, close your eyes and sleep, because you got important work tomorrow."

"Kind of like what I did last night with Elizabeth, Gabe. I like that story."

"In the morning son, they'll blow reveille—loud and fast. You'd have to be a dying elephant not to jump up at reveille. New day, new orders."

"I like that story Gabe, thanks frien'."

"So, here's your reveille for today, son. You go do what it is you're doing, then, when it's time, you blow taps because at eight o'clock tonight you need to be on the top of Lily Cup's building in the quarter."

"Ol' man, can it be tomorrow night?"

"Why not tonight, son?"

"I'm still tracking today."

"Promise me son, you'll blow reveille in the morning tomorrow and taps late tomorrow to shut it down so you can be there?"

"I promise, frien'—from now on I'll always blow taps to stop for the day—rest the brain. Starting tomorrow, dass for true."

"Tomorrow night it is then—we'll all be there looking fancy, so dress up cause we're going to have the biggest welcome home party for you ever. Sasha got her a new dress to dance in and she'll be modeling it."

"It's not a date," Peck said.

"It's not a date, son, but can you blow taps for yourself in time to quit for the day and be on that rooftop tomorrow night at eight to see old friends?"

"That's a metaphor, Gabe?"

"Think it is, son—never sure."

"I can and I will. I promise. See you all tomorrow night on Lily Cup's rooftop."

23.

AS PECK WALKED INTO THE MORTUARY, he saw Larry and Chris standing over a body of a woman on one of the tables.

"How you all are, friens'?"

"Good to see you again, Peck," Chris said.

Larry put an arm around Peck's neck and kissed him on the forehead.

"Welcome back, son."

"The lady on the table, Chris—why's her head covered?" Peck asked.

"I had to remove the parietal in order to get the bullet out, Peck. It's not pretty. Let's keep it covered."

"What is that—how you say—parietal thing, Chris?" Peck asked.

"It's the top part of the skull, Peck."

"Why would a bullet hit someone on top of the head, Chris?" Larry asked.

"I'm questioning that, myself," Chris said.

"In a swamp or bayou, Chris, I could—how you say—skip mussel shells on top of the water. I don't know bullets, though."

"Ricochet," Chris said.

"Hanh?" Peck asked.

"It ricocheted off something and hit her?" Larry asked.

"Peck's amazing, Lieutenant. He's right with his swamp scenario and the mussel shells."

"Why are you so sure, Chris—that it was a ricochet?" Larry asked.

"The bullet is brass, Lieutenant."

"And that means?" Larry asked.

"The brass bullet had lead fragments on its face, Lieutenant. Lead in bullets will mushroom typically but not splinter and get in front of the brass cover."

"You're right."

"This bullet hit something lead."

"I'll be damned," Larry said.

"It hit something lead, Lieutenant, ricocheted and then hit our burglar from above."

"Not many products, other than bullets, have lead in them nowadays, Chris. What's your guess?"

"Don't move," Chris said.

Chris rushed from the table, pulling his rubber gloves off. He picked up a file folder and hurried back.

"Let's see photos I took of the store's interior, gentlemen."

He dealt the prints like he was dealing cards, impatiently waiting for the right photo to come up.

"Here—exactly," Chris said.

"What are you looking at?" Larry asked.

From the ceiling, Lieutenant. That's a Tiffany lamp hanging. This store 'D and A' is diamonds and antiques. You even bought a desk lamp there, Lieutenant."

"I did."

"There was a time—Depression, war—when the cost of brass was so high that some parts in Tiffany lamps were made using lead."

Chris pointed to the Tiffany lamp in the photo.

"If we check that lamp suspended from the ceiling over the body—I'm certain you'll find that the bullet hit it and ricocheted and entered Marilyn's parietal lobe—from above."

"*Aye yi-yi*," Peck said.

"Death is like a swamp, Peck. It's inevitable but the mystery for us is in finding out how and why," Chris said.

"You had a reason for me to come today," Peck said.

"You wanted to go back ten and forward ten, Peck. To see if there's a connection to your pickup explosion. This burglary was about 3:45 this morning," Larry said.

"So her shooting was an accident, maybe," Peck said.

"This is a real mystery thriller, Peck. This lady was shot inside a diamond and antique store."

"Chris already said that, Larry. Did a burglar shoot while holding her up?"

"That's just it—the dead woman was the burglar, Peck. She was shot in the act by a blind girl."

"*Aye yi-yi!*"

"Hear this—the blind girl doesn't know she hit anyone with the gun. She shot at sounds—thinks she just scared them off. She hit the walls twice, a storefront window twice and another window once. Now maybe even a ceiling lamp."

"I can imagine it," Peck said.

"You can?" Chris asked.

"Were there bullet holes in places, Chris?"

"There were two holes in the front glass—bulletproof so they wouldn't shatter. There was a two-foot pane over the door near the ceiling. It was a blue stained glass, like in a church. Probably been over the door for a century. The entire glass from that window shattered and fell from the frame and crashed on the sidewalk outside by the door."

"A blind person has hearing like the best of animals, Larry. A blind person doesn't have lazy ears," Peck said.

"Didn't I tell you we needed him in on this?" Larry asked. "Talk to me Peck."

"They have a good sense of touch too. At 3:45 in the morning, she was scared—her adrenalin kicked in—she shot around sounds she heard. Wanted to scare them—where'd she come from, Larry?"

"From the apartment upstairs."

"She turned around fast after shooting—I'm thinking with her hitting a window she could hear outside traffic noises, street sounds and maybe thought the burglar had run outside, left the store. She probably bumped into something trying to leave the room and knew she had to concentrate her own self on not tripping or bumping into other things and didn't hear the body fall."

"I found the gun on the floor by the stairs, Peck," Chris said.

"Something knocked it out of her hand, she became—how you say—distracted and she ran upstairs and locked the door upstairs. Did she call 911?"

"She did," Chris said.

"Lucky for us, Officer Downs was in the area," Larry said. "He saw the body through the door window, knew I wanted in on it. He didn't call dispatch, he called Chris."

"He didn't call me on this one, you did," Peck said.

"He's off for two days. What's in your head, son?" Larry asked.

"It's in the stars," Peck said. "Larry, you think maybe this is connected to my pickup blowing up."

"It has that smell, Peck—just a hunch."

"Tell me why you're thinking it is," Peck said.

"Listen to this one, Peck. Chris learned that the blind girl is the daughter of the diamond and antique store owner."

"Okay."

"She told him her father closed the store for three days and was on a short cruise—"

"Okay."

"He was going to propose to his girlfriend on the cruise."

"Okay."

"She came from Jackson where she lives with her mother, to keep his parrot company. The store would stay closed while he was gone on the cruise."

"How do you see a connection, Larry?" Peck asked.

"The store owner is still on the cruise. His girlfriend he was going to propose to was a Marilyn Knotts."

"Okay," Peck said. "And—?

"Look at the toe tag on our lady here, Peck"

Peck stepped to the end of the table and touched the tag wired to the toe of the cadaver.

"Marilyn Knotts," Peck whispered. He turned around, staring at a medical equipment cabinet on a distant wall.

"What are you thinking now, Peck?" Larry asked.

"It's all connected somehow—but unlike my dead man, this Marilyn Knotts here doesn't have a husband."

"She only has a boyfriend who's on a cruise," Chris said.

"Maybe he's not on a cruise," Peck said.

"Are you thinking she was set up?"

"I'm just thinking, frien'."

Chris showed Peck the pictures he had taken and explained the invisible ink, the circles and the *x's* on the glass. He explained that the corpse had a set of keys to the display case but broke the glass on top with a ball peen hammer and took two expensive Rolex watches. Peck took it all in, tweaking his chin with his finger and thumb.

"What's on your mind, son?"

"Except for the fact this dead lady here broke the glass and took watches, this is not an inside job, I'm thinking."

"Talk to me, Peck."

"One—if the owner was not on a cruise but he was kidnapped, he'll be back tomorrow like the wife in the other case I'm working on. His girlfriend is dead, no use anymore. Same—how you say—MO."

"I see your point," Larry said.

"Two—if he is on the cruise and she was supposed to be with him, he maybe just got mad that she didn't show up when they were supposed to board—broke up with her—

and he went on the cruise anyway. He paid for it. Maybe not—how you say—refundable."

"I agree with that," Larry said.

"Three—if he comes back and tells us this lady—how you say—stood him up, but she called him minutes before the sailing time to tell him she couldn't go—maybe she had a brother or sister or frien' or something in trouble and she was made to do this thing … steal the watches like that. She was warned not to unlock the display case so it would look like a burglary and he could collect insurance."

"Or to make it look like an outside job," Larry said.

"Interesting," Chris said. "Sounds pretty much like you've wrapped this one up—you just have to see if you can tie the two together."

"There's another one," Peck said.

"Talk to me, son."

"The blind girl."

"You think that blind girl could have planned this? I hardly—" Larry started.

"She could have been a jealous daughter—her mamma betrayed by daddy—by this Marilyn, a bad—how you say—temptress."

"Jesus," Larry said.

"Amazing," Chris said.

Peck leaned in close to the body of Marilyn Knotts.

"Maybe not," Peck said. "Maybe not number four."

"What now?" Larry asked.

"I didn't smell anything. No perfume, powder, no cologne."

"Which tells you what, son?"

"A blind person can smell good, Larry. The blind girl couldn't have known who she was—no smells. The blind girl is innocent, with one exception."

"Which is?" Larry asked.

"You only have the blind girl's word that this Marilyn lady didn't answer when she called out for who was in the room."

Chris nodded in surprise.

"She would have known her voice," Peck said. "But I'm ruling that out too."

"I think that could be a possibility, Peck. Why would you rule out the blind girl recognizing the voice?" Chris asked.

"Because when Patricia ax who was in the room, all this lady had to do was say something like—how you say—'No worries, Patricia—it's only me. Your daddy sent me in for something.' If the blind girl wasn't upset about her daddy leaving her mother, she wouldn't have shot then."

"Unless she wanted to murder her," Chris said.

"Exactly," Peck said. "But if she did shoot the gun, it wouldn't have been all over the place with this dead lady looking at her, talking to her. Bullet holes would be grouped."

"We're wasting time, guys. What's next, Peck?" Larry asked.

"I'm going to Mrs. Bergeron's, take her to the station and ax her things. Larry, can you get me an address and what you can learn about this Marilyn lady's family?"

"I'll have it later today."

"Make it tomorrow, Larry. Let's wait and see if cruise man comes back and if he does, what he has to say."

"Are you doing Charlie's Blue Note tonight, Peck? Lily Cup would love to see you. Nobody's seen you since your pickup exploded."

"Not tonight, cher. I'm working."

"Are you really working tonight, son?"

"I'm doing jambalaya—but I'm working, dass for true."

Peck left the morgue and climbed into his pickup. He called Aurelie at the phone store.

"Hi," Aurelie said.

"We still on tonight, bébé?"

"Yes, if you're up to it."

"You sure you want to put up with me?"

"I've got everything you asked for on those calls."

"Ah, so good."

"And I bought a new dress to dance Dixieland. I want to model it for you. I have the jambalaya done—I just have to heat it. Do you play poker, Peck?"

"My frien' Gabe teached me five card stud, why?"

"Are you daring, Peck?"

"I'm daring, cher."

"Good. jambalaya and red wine put me in a naughty mood. The girls across the hall are from Memphis. They sometimes have parties if we get bored."

"Nah-nah, we won't get bored, bébé. Moods can pass a good time. Don't need to be daring for parties, cher."

"They play strip poker at their parties."

"Ah oui—that might take—how you say—daring. Text me an address. I'll come after I shower at our shotgun."

"You can shower at my place, Peck. Gotta' go now. Back inside—to work. See you later."

24.

AS PECK DROVE to Magazine Street, he called Christie Bergeron's phone.

"Hello?"

"Christie, this is Peck."

"Oh, hello."

"I wanted to see if you think you're ready to talk with me, bébé—so we can solve this thing."

"I'm ready."

"Can I come over?"

"I don't want to talk in front of the children."

"I'll pick you up. We'll go someplace to talk."

"Can you give me an hour to find a babysitter?"

"Can you afford a babysitter, Christie?"

"Give me an hour and pick me up."

"Watch for me, I'll pull up out front in an hour."

"Okay."

Peck ended the call as his phone rang. It was Lily Cup.

"Hello?" Peck asked.

"I got an invitation to Elizabeth's graduation from cooking school, Peck. I called her to thank her but had to decline. She told me she's moving to Paris," Lily Cup said.

"Ah *oui*."

"Are you going to Paris with her, Peck?"

"Two little kids and their momma want to find out what happened to their daddy. I'm tracking, is all. I have to concentrate. I've got to go now, cher. People I need to call."

Peck clicked off and answered a call from Larry.

"How you all are, Larry?"

"I have both you and Lieutenant Gaines on the same call, Peck. It's called a conference call," Chris said.

"Ah okay."

"Talk to us, Chris," Larry said.

"Autopsy of our Marilyn Knotts reveals a diamond ring in her stomach. She swallows a ring. The plot thickens."

"*Aye yi-yi!*" Peck said. "That locks one up, dass for true."

"Locks what up, Peck? Talk to me."

"Not now, Larry. I'm tracking."

"This is getting heavy," Larry said. "Peck, what are you working on? What are you holding back?"

"I'm in a swamp, Larry. Morning moon with a red sky. I need a clear head all day. I'll tell you what I got later. Right now, I'm picking Mrs. Bergeron up and taking her to the precinct room so we can talk. Tonight, I'm meeting someone who has important things for me to see. I'll come see you and Chris in the morning."

"Call me first, son."

"Why?"

"So, I'll know when you're coming and I can meet you there. Jesus, Peck, you're a tough cookie."

"Don't mind the lieutenant, Peck—he hasn't had his morning chicory," Chris said.

"Thanks, Chris. Thanks for this news on the—how you say—the conference thing," Peck said.

"Go get 'em, Peck," Chris said.

25.

PECK PULLED IN FRONT of the shotgun on Magazine Street. Christie saw him drive up and came out. She closed the wrought iron gate behind her and climbed into his pickup.

"How you all are, Christie?"

"I'm still in shock about losing Anthony. We had a pact that we'd live to be old and move to an island somewhere."

"A *oui*—I know about dreams, cher … so sad."

"The kids are doing better—they miss their daddy."

"He was a good daddy. I could tell, listening to your little girl."

"Did you go for your read, Peck?"

"I did—my frien' in Baton Rouge just got a job as a chef—she's moving to Paris to cook creole in a jazz café there."

"Anthony always wanted to play jazz in Paris."

"The lieutenant is letting us use a room at the precinct so we can talk. Is that okay, cher—or would you rather go some other place?"

"That'll be fine."

Peck pulled into the precinct parking and turned his phone off.

"Keep your phone on because of the kids, cher."

"That's considerate of you, Peck. Thank you. I'll set it to vibrate so it won't distract us."

Peck walked her into the station, introduced himself to the desk sergeant and asked for marker pens. He asked if they had large pads of paper so they could keep notes. They had supplies. He walked Christie to the third room where they sat across the table from each other. Peck reached and held her hand.

"I know it ain't easy, these times, but you're going to make it, cher."

"I'll get through it—I'm strong. I'll see the kids stay strong. We'll be okay. It'll be better when I find steady work."

"Let me tell you why we're here," Peck said. "Here's how I track—you understand track?"

"I do. You're a detective."

"Sometimes, Christie, when you hunt it's good if you stand and think before you go into the swamp. You stand and think of why you're hunting. They can only be two things you hunting for, cher. It's good if you think about which."

"Only two?"

"You hunting for something to sell to the market or you hunt so you can eat today."

"So, are you saying it's a matter of urgency if you're hunting to put food on the table today?"

"That's right."

"I don't quite understand, Peck. In both instances you're hunting for food, aren't you?"

"The difference is if you're hungry you know to look bigger than just the sights and sounds and movements, that's all. When you're hunting for market, you let the prey find you—with noises, movements, like that."

"So, when you're hungry and you have to put food on the table you don't wait for things to find you. You look to find them first?" Christie asked.

"You're a good tracker, cher. You're smart."

"I was married to a musician, Peck. Anthony wrote music and he taught me about sounds—when they were important and when silence was better."

"Ah *oui*, but remember one thing."

"What's that?"

"You said 'was married', cher. You're still married to that good man and good daddy. He will be in your heart, forever."

Christie teared up.

"Christie, a week before you were kidnapped, what were you doing?"

"I was going to job interviews. I was changing diapers. I was sewing."

"Sewing? What were you sewing?"

"I'd make bow ties for Anthony to wear while he was performing. He loved my bow ties. He'd sometimes autograph them and give them to fans who showed their appreciation with big tips."

"Tell me about your job interviews."

"There was one at the Visitor's Center, but it was a lot of calling people and I'm pretty shy—not comfortable doing telemarketing. That's what they call it."

"I see."

"There was the company that canned coffee— chicory actually. I didn't know the accounting software well enough for that job. The hours were not good for Anthony and my schedules. The job I really wanted was with Judge Chandler. He was so nice. He respected mothers who supported their husbands and who worked to help out. He understood that children needed special attention from time to time. He loved music—we talked about the music Anthony was trying to write—how we saved for years to get the perfect piano for our house so he could write his music."

"Cher, did they knock on your door, or did they ring the doorbell?"

"Who?"

"The day you were kidnapped, did they knock on the door or ring the bell?"

"They rang the bell."

"When you opened the door, did they say anything?"

"No."

"Did you say anything?"

"I don't remember. One of them grabbed my arm and pulled me outside."

"What did you see?"

"They had stockings over their heads."

"Were they white, black? Could you see?"

"I don't remember. They were wearing gloves. They pulled me fast."

"What could you see?"

"I saw a truck."

"What else?"

"I remember seeing the numbers 784."

"On the truck?"

"Somewhere on it, yes—I don't remember where."

"Was it a big truck? A small truck?"

"It was a truck like a painter or carpenter would use."

"Like a delivery truck, cher. A van, maybe?"

"That's it—a delivery truck. No windows, I remember that. It had no windows on the sides."

"You told me before, they taped your eyes."

"Yes."

"At your door?"

"No, when they pushed me in the truck. When I was inside, one of them taped my eyes, one of them taped my wrists together."

"Was the truck moving while they were taping you?"

"Yes. I remember falling into someone."

"Were you standing?"

"No, I was on my knees but I lost my balance. I think the truck turned and I fell over."

"Cher, can you remember if you fell to your right or to your left? Do you remember?"

"I fell to my left. I remember falling to my left."

"Do you remember, when you fell over—were you facing the front of the truck or the back of the truck?"

"The back, I'm sure. I saw them close the back door before they taped my eyes. Why is that important?"

"The way you fell will tell us which way they turned—and we can track the direction they took you."

"I fell to my left—I was facing the back doors."

"Inside that truck, cher—what stands out in your mind? Not the people, not the motions, not the—how you say—fear in your heart. What stood out? Something you remember in your nightmares of this whole thing?"

"The smell."

"You remember the smell?"

"I could smell bread."

"You could smell bread. This is good."

"It was like it smells when you go into a small bakery. Could be cookies baking. It could be cakes in ovens—the French breads, everything has a special smell of flour and sugar."

"My frien' Gabe bakes bread. I know the smell."

"Tell me about your reading, Peck."

"Ah *oui*. Sorry."

"Did you pull a card for me, Peck?"

"Your card was the Eight of Swords."

"Oh God."

"Audrey says the Eight of Swords means—how you say—abandonment. She thinks you were kidnapped to appear you were walking away from your family and responsibilities. Anthony, your husband and those kids' daddy were led to believe you left and would only come back if he was ready to make a sacrifice."

"Are you saying they kidnapped me to get him to do something, like a sacrifice?"

"Ah *oui*. That's what I'm thinking. Audrey, the reader too. She thinks that too."

Christie lifted a tissue from her purse.

"Aw, cher—I can tell you one thing for certain."

"What?"

"That man never once thought you—how you say—that abandonment thing. He knew you were taken. I bet they told him. He knew what he had to do to get you back. Don't you ever not believe the bad things he was going through in his brain with you gone. Never."

"Thank you."

"You told me about a computer talking to you—how you say—to keep quiet or they will kill your babies."

"Yes."

"What do you remember about the ride in the truck?"

"I remember that when it felt like it slowed down it turned in somewhere and it was a lot of bumps until it stopped. I remember them taking me out and walking to a garage or shed or something, and they locked me inside. The computer voice told me there were cameras inside and if I took the tape off my eyes, they would kill my babies."

"*Aye yi-yi.*"

"Somebody brought food. My wrists were taped but they put a sandwich in my hand and stayed with me until I finished eating it. One time I told them I didn't want to eat and someone slapped my face. I remember they didn't say a word, they just slapped my face like it was a warning. I ate the sandwich. Then I could hear the padlock close outside the door."

"Do you remember hearing anything else?"

"I remember one thing. I remember a voice saying, "Where's the Lord—bring the Lord in.""

"Was that like a religious thing, you think, cher?"

"I don't know. It was a woman's voice, I think. It was like she was upset."

"Christie, this is so good, everything you've told me. We'll take a break now. You go be with your babies and I'll do some tracking. I'll take you home. We can do this again tomorrow morning, okay?"

"That'll be fine. Have I helped at all?"

"Ah *oui*—I learned so much from you, cher. Let it all—how you say—settle in my brain. Tomorrow we'll do more and maybe have answers soon, I'm purdy sure."

Peck drove Christie to her door on Magazine Street.

"Hug the babies," Peck said.

"I'll see you in the morning, Peck. Text me when you know when. I'll get a sitter. Thank you for caring."

Peck watched Christie get out and waited until she was inside the house before driving off. He touched Larry's contact number on his phone.

"Talk to me," Larry said.

"Larry, can I ax a special thing? Something maybe you can make happen?"

"Sure, son."

"Can you maybe get somebody like at a funeral home—you know those people who can make a dead body look good—can you maybe—?"

"You want to have Mr. Bergeron's face look normal and not burned off … am I right son?"

"Ah *oui*, dass for true."

"I'll make it happen, son. I'll let you know when."

"Thank you, Larry. You're a good frien'."

26.

PECK WALKED IN THE MORGUE unannounced and found Larry and Chris chatting.

"You said if we need to meet you would call me, Peck," Larry said.

"I came to see Chris, but you're here, so that's good—dass for true."

"You just can't pop up anytime you feel a whim."

"When a pirogue comes too close to a cypress—" Peck started.

Larry looked at his watch.

"Peck, my friend, we love you but save the metaphors. I had no idea you were coming, and I've got the police commissioner waiting on me at Antoine's. Talk to us."

"Can I see the ring, Chris—the ring your autopsy found in the dead lady's stomach?"

Chris opened a locked toolbox and lifted out a plastic container. He handed it to Peck.

"Here."

"Okay, good," Peck said.

"Talk to us, Peck," Larry said.

"Is this an expensive ring?"

"Ten carats. We estimate at least a hundred thousand dollars," Chris said.

"*Aye yi-yi*," Peck said.

"It's a keeper," Chris said.

Peck walked to the table where the corpse lay.

"This dead lady was in the Maple Street store when it was robbed," Peck said.

"Our Marilyn Knotts here?" Chris asked.

"She was?" Larry asked.

"This is her."

"You know for certain?" Larry asked.

"I know, Larry. I know for certain."

"I thought there was no visual ID on the woman in the Maple Street jewelry store robbery, Peck." Larry said.

"There wasn't. Dass for true."

"So how can you pin it on her? A hoody ran in, did a snatch and grab and ran out."

"Nobody ran in that store on Maple to take anything," Peck said.

"Slow down, Peck, what are you saying?"

"The person who ran in the store only ran in to make it look like they took something. It was this lady here, the same one who stole the Rolex watches on Hampson. She was at that place. When the person ran in and pretended to grab it from her, she swallowed this ring. She was looking at it with that—how you say—eye thing, but when the person reached for her face, she swallowed the ring. She was the one who stole the diamond ring, not the runner. Chris's autopsy of the dead lady found the ring, Larry."

"Pretty impressive, son—if you can prove it. Tell us what backup you've got."

"Other than a ring being in her stomach?"

"What more do you have, son?"

Peck took the printouts Maizie had given him out of an envelope.

"Here."

Peck spread the printouts on a table.

"And here … and here ... and here."

"What it's looking like," Peck started, "The runner who came into the store and our dead lady here are in—how you say—cahoots. They're a team."

"They were working together?" Chris asked.

"They may have been working together, but I'm thinking maybe somebody else is working them," Peck said.

"Like your pickup thief, Peck? Is that where your head is?" Larry asked.

"Chris?" Peck asked. "Why would a store manager who was about to go on an expensive cruise and get engaged to the owner of the whole store and all them expensive watches go in and steal two watches—and in the middle of the night too. Why?"

"Doesn't make sense, her stealing," Chris said. "She marries the guy and she'll own it all—all the watches."

"Unless she was forced?" Larry asked.

"Like Peck's pickup thief?" Chris asked.

"Sounds like Peck has found us a link," Larry said.

Larry's phone rang, interrupting him. He stepped away to talk.

"Chris," Peck said. "This ring ties things together. Can you have Forensics dust anything our dead lady might have touched in the Maple Street store to prove it was her in there?"

"I will, Peck."

"You have her ID, Chris?"

"We do."

"How about you tell the snobby Paul Robert her name. See if he will admit knowing her."

"Good job, Peck."

"I have another idea, Chris. Maybe think on it."

"Tell me, Peck."

"Larry was funnin' my pirogue metaphor but—"

"Peck you have one of the keenest, most observant minds I've ever seen. I listen to Peck Finch. Tell me."

"Okay. Let's not tell that jewelry store on Maple about the ring. Let's not let on we know anything about it. Don't tell them that this dead lady was killed in another store. I want to see if anything fits together before we let a cat—how you say—?"

"Let the cat out of the bag, Peck?" Chris mused. "Before we let the cat out of the bag?"

"'Xactly, Chris, thank you."

Just as Peck and Chris were shaking on it, Larry walked up.

"Clear your morning calendar, Peck," Larry said.

"How's that?" Peck asked.

"That was Officer Downs. Been told that our D & A Jewelry and Fine Antiques owner has showed his face."

"Back from his cruise, Lieutenant?" Chris asked.

Peck interrupted sarcastically.

"Chris, don't be making no assumptions. You know by now our good lieutenant here don't interrogate people over the phone. He has to see the pupils in a man's eyes— like in a swamp afore he learns anything." Peck guffawed.

"From a pirogue," Chris jibed.

"Okay, wise asses—our jewelry store owner is back," Larry said. "He knows a burglar was shot and killed in his store—a rug was soaked in blood, for Christ's sake— and he knows his daughter likely fired the shot that killed the burglar. He also knows the daughter was not a person of interest in the case and is free to go home to Mississippi. I'll have him in Interrogation Room Three tomorrow at nine a.m."

"I need room three tomorrow morning," Peck said.

"Better use it tonight. Big things in the morning, son. Be there tomorrow," Larry said. "Nine a.m."

"What time is it now?" Peck asked.

"Six p.m. Why?" Larry asked.

"I already—how you say—blew 'taps' Larry. I can't hear anything you saying."

"What!?" Larry barked.

"Talk to your brother, Gabe, Lieutenant. I'm enjoying jambalaya tonight and maybe some poker with— how you say—an informant. Tomorrow night I'll be going to my billet at the shotgun. I'll get looking purdy and meet you on top of Lily Cup's building at eight. The building roof was your orders, Larry … the taps thing was Gabe's idea. I'm all done thinking for the day … sorry."

"Pretty full of yourself, aren't you, son?"

"This is my case, Lieutenant," Peck replied sarcastically. "Kindly tell Mr. D & A it'll have to be another time. I have a meeting with Maizie in the morning—after I go to Mass."

"You have a meeting and you don't want me, a police lieutenant, in the room with you—is that what you're saying, Peck? And who the hell is Maizie?"

As if ignoring Larry, Peck turned to Chris.

"Chris, taps have blown for me today. I've got an important thing to do tonight. Did you hear something, Chris? Anything? Somebody talking?" Peck asked, referencing Larry's voice.

"I didn't hear anything, Peck," Chris replied. "I can smell the jambalaya already."

"Chris, tell the prince here I'll put it off a day—but that's it?" Larry asked.

Peck grinned a victory grin and walked out.

"I need a drink," Larry said.

27.

AURELIE'S APARTMENT BUILDING was once a grand manor in the Garden District. It was four stories with a grace of the turn of the twentieth century. It had been tastefully transposed into an apartment house, with several small apartments on each floor. The fourth floor was one apartment, a small room with pitched ceilings and a floor-to-ceiling walk-through window with a curved balcony. When he knocked on a third-floor apartment door, a girl wearing a man's sweatshirt that hung down to her thighs in bare feet opened the door.

"Hi, I was just leaving."

"Hi," Peck said.

The girl turned to Aurelie.

"You're right. He's cute."

"You from Memphis, bébé?" Peck asked.

"Sure am, you been there?"

"Peabody Hotel and I danced on Beale Street—dass for true. I like Memphis."

"You an Elvis fan?"

"I don't know too much about all that—how you say—rock and roll things."

"He's so cute, Aurelie. Y'all come over if you get bored."

Peck grinned and pulled the door after she stepped out.

"That was Kala," Aurelie said. "We've been friends for a long time. We moved in on the same day."

"She seems nice."

"We can go over later if you want, Peck. Her place is a little bigger than this and Kala has a poker game just for fun."

"Strip poker, bébé?"

"Sometimes—if the girls arrange a hunk like you to join in. Usually, they play for pistachios."

Peck smiled and stepped into the corner kitchen.

"Oh my, cher, this jambalaya smells so good, dass for true."

"It's from an old family recipe. We have time to talk before it's heated."

Aurelie poured two glasses of red wine. She handed one to Peck.

"Sit on the sofa, I'll show you what I've got."

She brought in a paper shopping bag where she had papers camouflaged under several folded newspapers.

"Whose phone first, Peck? Christie or Anthony Bergeron?"

"Let's do Christie first."

Aurelie handed Peck three monthly statements from Christie's cell phone. She had highlighted repeated numbers in different colors.

"Do you know who she called?"

"Most calls are just regular calls, like to schools, grocery stores, pizza delivery. That kind of thing. Nothing stands out."

"She's a substitute teacher, I remember."

"Three are either to or from a coffee company. Five were to or from the New Orleans Convention and Visitors people."

"She was trying to get a job."

"Four are to or from the criminal court house—the one downtown."

Peck lifted a small pad out of his pocket and turned some pages.

"The court house, bébé—was the number at the courthouse for a Judge Chandler?"

Aurelie lifted the statement page to look at her notes.

"Can't really tell. That number was blocked by the courthouse switchboard. They'll do that for security reasons,

I guess. I was afraid to call it to find out in case they tracked incoming calls. It probably means it's someone important, like a judge."

"Let's look at Anthony's phone," Peck said.

"Anthony's phone doesn't make a lot of calls or texts. He has high data charges but very few calls."

"What does—how you say—data charges mean, bébé?"

"Data means he used his phone to look up things on the internet—like you use it to look up word definitions, Peck."

"Ah *oui*."

"That's called *data*."

"Anything—how you say—unusual that stands out with his calls?"

"One number does."

"What number?"

"This one. It's from a Lillian Meyer's phone."

"What do you think is interesting about that number, frien'?"

"Eight calls, Peck."

"Are they lovers, maybe?"

"If they are, Lillian Meyer is pursuing him."

"How's that?"

"He's never called her once. She called him eight times."

"Interesting."

"Are you pleased, Peck?"

"You did so good, cher. *Merci*."

"Would you like me to model my new dress before I serve the jambalaya?"

"Ah *oui*."

Aurelie took a box from a side table.

"I have two dresses. I don't know which I like better. I'll model them both and you pick the one you like. I'll return the other."

"Okay."

Aurelie stood, turned her back to Peck, dropped her shorts to the floor and pulled the T-shirt up over her head and off. The first dress she put on was a navy-blue blazer dress with a double-breasted look and large brass buttons.

"Oh, I like that one, cher—dass for true."

"I wouldn't wear a bra with this dress, so you wouldn't see the straps like you can now."

"I like it, cher."

"Hold on," Aurelie said.

She pulled it up over her head and put the next one on.

"This other one is a baby doll dress. It's popular for sexy nights."

"Ah *oui*—so good."

"Which do you like, Peck? When we go dancing, which do you like best?"

"This is so … so … Let me ax cher, what is your budget?"

"Ha ha! You are such a man. Looking nice is not about money, honey."

"Then get both."

"Huh?"

"The—how you say—Baby Doll one for dancing slow jazz and Dixieland. The other one—"

"This blazer dress?"

"Yes—that one is elegant—is that the word? For dinner in Commander's Palace or at the Columns, cher, for eating shrimp and grits and watching the streetcars go by."

Peck stood up. Aurelie took both his hands in hers.

"Did I do good for you, Peck?"

"You did so good, cher."

She leaned over and kissed him a quick kiss on the lips. She leaned back.

"There—paid in full," Aurelie whispered.

The evening was restful for Peck and fulfilling for Aurelie, being able to entertain and show her human side outside of the work environment.

They spoke of seasonings, which hot sauce was best on what foods. Peck shared what Leah Chase said about never putting hot sauce on gumbo—it just wasn't done. Aurelie spoke of her childhood in Church Point and occasional visits with her grandparents—*Momo* and *Pépére*. Peck spoke of his youth in Carencro and what the best bait was for his snoods when he cast for fish to trade with the fish and egg man at the market for eggs or a few dollars. He demonstrated knife sharpening using the shell of an uncooked egg. Peck told about investigating for Lily Cup sometimes and Larry sometimes.

Aurelie followed the jambalaya with homemade raisin bread pudding and a butter syrup topping.

"Aurelie, can I ax you something?"

"Anything, Peck."

"Can I stay tonight?"

"Here? With me?"

"Here, anyway. I just got too much on my brain to go home tonight. I'm trying to solve some things and maybe could have more questions to ax."

"I've been watching you, Peck."

"You have?"

"You amaze me with how you investigate. Those people are lucky to have you, I'll say."

"So?"

"You'll have to sleep in my bed. The sofa is too small."

Peck helped clear the table and washed the dishes in the sink. He'd hand each to Aurelie to dry with a cloth towel. When finished she walked toward the bed.

"We can go across the hall and play poker, or we go to bed, Peck. Your choice."

Peck pulled his T-shirt up over his head. Unbuckled and dropped his jeans to the floor and kicked them off while standing in tight briefs. Aurelie checked his package and smiled. She pulled her sweater over her head and off. Unsnapped her bra and dropped it. Unbuttoned her shorts and dropped them and jumped into bed in panties.

"Which side you like, Peck?"

"Any side, cher—what do you like best, bébé?"

"I like 'top'." Aurelie guffawed.

Peck grinned and crawled in beside her, his arm over her pulling her to him. She snuggled her head on his chest.

"If you get any ideas, Peck—just ask," Aurelie whispered.

"I have one, cher."

"One's a good start—ha ha. Tell me."

"About that Lillian Meyer, you told me—you know calls to Anthony from her?"

"I remember. What about her?"

"You think you can find me where she lives?"

"Tomorrow I maybe can."

"Thanks, cher."

"Go to sleep, Peck. Your brain is elsewhere tonight."

"This was so much fun, cher. The dinner was the best. We'll go dancing so you can wear your purdy dress—I promise."

They dozed off.

28.

A SIREN DOWN ON THE STREET awoke Peck. Aurelie lifted her head from the pillow.

"You okay?" Aurelie whispered.

"Cher, what time is it?"

Aurelie looked at her cell phone.

"It's 9:45, why?"

"Nine forty-five is too early to be in bed, cher. Put the purdy dress on—the new one. We're going to Charlie's Blue Note."

"Are you serious?"

"Get dressed, cher, if you want to dance. I have to see somebody too. So I may do some tracking."

Aurelie jumped up and grabbed clothes. She fastened her bra and slipped into the Baby Doll dress. It was soon they were walking into the alley leading to Charlie's Blue Note. The mellow *vaaaaaaa…vaaaaaaa…veee* of a tenor sax welcomed them into the room. The dance floor was busy. Peck saw his friend, André, sitting at the bar. There were two empty stools.

"Let's sit at the bar, cher."

"Where you at, my friend?" Charlie asked.

"How you all are, Charlie—André. Just come to dance with a frien'. Gentlemen meet Miss Aurelie here. She's helping me with a case."

"Welcome to Charlie's Blue Note," Charlie said. "Charlie was my daddy, but it's my bar—named after my daddy."

"Hello Charlie," Aurelie said.

"Peck," André said. "If this pretty girl here helping you with a case—girl you're working with a winner here, I'll tell you that. Charlie let me buy Peck and this pretty girl a drink."

"Thank you, Mr. André," Aurelie said. "I'm pleased to meet you."

"André there are three seats. Can you sit in the middle cause I have to ax you something, you know?"

"Of course, bébé, but you ain't going to ask André here nothing until you dance with the pretty girl. If you don't dance with the lady, I'm going to."

Peck smiled and took Aurelie's hand and pulled her to him as they danced onto the floor. André moved to the middle of the three stools.

The band was playing a slow riff of Louis Armstrong blues with a jazz twist and turn here and there. Peck and Aurelie's bodies were in sync—they glided as if they had danced together before.

"You come here often?" Aurelie asked.

"Purdy much, cher. My frien's meet here to dance. They have a rule no business talk here. But seems all I do is business talk."

"I like how you dance, Peck."

"Thanks, cher."

"I like how you hold me."

"You okay if I ax André things? He may could help me."

"You're an investigator, Peck. I'm so okay with you doing what you have to do. I'm fine with it."

When the dance was finished, they walked back to the bar. Seeing them, Charlie jumped over the bar and approached Peck.

"Excuse me, bébé. I need Peck a minute—just a second," Charlie said.

"That's fine," Aurelie said. She sat up on the stool to André's right.

Charlie pulled Peck into the back room and gave him a big embrace.

"You don't know how good it is to see you alive. You can't imagine what we all thought when your pickup exploded. I saw the flames. I love you my friend, don't you ever forget that."

Peck returned the hug.

"Thank you my good frien'—but if you kiss me, I'm going to have a lot of explaining to do."

They ended their embrace with a guffaw and returned to the bar. Charlie jumped up on the bar and got behind it.

"You two want you some red beans and rice?" Charlie asked.

"Charlie, this lady made the best jambalaya I had since Dooky Chase. We're full."

André leaned in Peck's direction.

"What's on that thinkin' mind of yours, my friend? You know you can always talk to André."

"André, you knew my truck blew up, right?"

"Don't waste André's time with bad questions, my friend."

"Sorry—but you may have thought it was those—how you say—traffickers—was the reason it exploded. But it wasn't."

"André didn't know that, son. Tell me your story—I will listen."

"Mr. André, it was the traffickers what set the bomb, but a long time ago. The hail made it go off—and a man trying to steal it got killed when it blowed up."

"A new twist, son?"

"André, I think somebody was making the man steal a pickup. Like blackmail."

"Tell me the story, son."

"The man's wife—the man who was killed when it blew up—his wife was kidnapped," Peck whispered. "They held her for three days, blindfolded. They didn't tell her why they kidnapped her—just drove her home one day, untied her hands and let her out with tape still on her eyes while they drove away."

"These are some bad people, Peck."

"Ah *oui*."

"So, you think she was kidnapped to make this man do something they wanted him to do so if anything went wrong, he would get caught and they would keep their hands clean?"

"Yes sir, André. I think that's how it went."

"What can André do for you, son?"

"I'm in the swamp. My pole taking me around the cypress, under the moss. I'm seeing the gators under a full morning moon, the crawfish snakes waiting and frogs jumping the wrong way sometimes and bein' supper. I see a lot of things, André. What am I not seeing?"

"Simple, my friend."

"It is? Oh, please tell me André, it's making me crazy in the head thinking about it."

"You're looking for things you're seeing my friend. Start looking for things you can't see."

"Hanh?"

André repeated himself.

"You're looking for things you can see, Peck. Start looking for things you can't see."

"I'll think on that, André. Thank you."

André turned toward Aurelie.

"Pretty girl, why don't you take this Cajun friend of André's home with you and make love with him so he can clear his brain?"

Aurelie's eyes widened as she grinned. Peck thanked André for the advice and the drinks. He promised he would think good on the advice. He drove Aurelie to her apartment building and parked.

"You still want to sleep over, Peck?"

"If you're okay with it, bébé."

"I'm fine with it."

"Don't let what André said embarrass you, Aurelie. He was just funnin'."

"A girl likes to be kissed, Peck. I'd like that—if you want to."

"I like kissing too, cher."

They climbed out of the pickup, held hands and went upstairs to Aurelie's apartment.

29.

IT WAS EIGHT IN THE MORNING when Peck woke up. Aurelie, in bra and panties, stood over the kitchen sink brushing her teeth.

"Good morning," Aurelie said.

"How late did we stay up, cher? How much wine did we drink?" Peck asked.

Aurelie spit into the sink, wiped her mouth with a paper towel and walked over to the bed with a dab of toothpaste on her finger. She sat on the bed and stuck her finger in his mouth with the toothpaste, as if to freshen his morning mouth.

"Two bottles of red—half bottle of chardonnay, and we kissed—oh we kissed—who could watch a clock?"

"It was fun, cher. Dass for true."

"Whoever you have waiting for you is one lucky girl, mister. You kiss good … so good."

"Well that sort of thing takes someone who appreciates—you know, cher?"

"Oh, I know," Aurelie said. She leaned over and kissed Peck, darting a toothpaste fresh tongue in and out in a morning tease.

"I don't know how I learned, bébé, I just like kissing."

"Oh, I do, Peck. I know the secret."

"You do? What secret?"

"You make a girl feel secure. You make her feel like you'll protect her—not try to take advantage, you know?"

"Ah *oui*. Not have to make sex, right?"

"Yes."

"Elizabeth taught me that. You'd like Elizabeth. She taught me good … when I was seventeen."

"Thank you, Elizabeth," Aurelie quipped.

"Cher, I have to go. I have something to do at the station."

Aurelie leaned in and gave Peck a lasting goodbye kiss, stood and started pulling clothes on.

"Lock the door when you leave, Peck. I have some morning shopping before I go into work at noon."

"I will, cher. Thanks for the jambalaya."

"Thanks for the dances, Peck."

"Ah *oui*."

"Call me," Aurelie said.

As Peck drove toward the precinct, he called Christie.

"Hi Peck," Christie said.

"How you are, cher?"

"I've been making notes for our next meeting, Peck. I'm better. I have a feeling that I'm getting my confidence back."

"That's so good, cher."

"That's the way Anthony would have wanted it. When are we meeting again?"

"Christie, I've got some errands to run. After, I'll call you, okay?"

"That'll be fine, Peck. I have some work this afternoon at a pre-school. I'm standing in for a pregnant teacher who has a doctor's appointment. The money's good."

"I'll text you when I'm ready, Christie. You just tell me when you can meet and I'll pick you up. Could be tomorrow too."

"Thank you for caring, Peck."

"That's what I do, cher. I care."

Peck walked in the precinct and up to the desk sergeant.

"Sergeant, you know if Maizie is in yet? Is she upstairs?"

"Nobody upstairs, Peck. A little early."

"Okay, Sergeant. If anyone is looking for me, tell them I went to church."

Peck left the precinct and drove to Jackson Square to get in a talk with God at the St. Louis Basilica. The church was dark inside but colorful stained-glass windows lit the way from his real world into the quiet calm of a private talk with the Lord, in His house. He genuflected upon entering and walked over to the vigil candles. He pulled two bills from his pocket and without looking at what they were, he pushed them in the *gift* slot. He sat in the front pew near the altar and kneeled in prayer. It was the window with the Sacred Heart that drew his attention today.

"Dear God, I'm sorry I'm so blessed with your spirit and guidance. Oh, I'm not sorry, because I have you in my life, God, and now my mamma's in my life again—but why I'm sorry this time it's because one nice man—he was a musician, a father and a husband, he got killed and now there's the other lady who's dead too. You are blessing me with help in solving them, I can feel it God—there's Audrey, she helps me think—there's Chris, he's a good help—and Maizie came and helped me too. I know you're doing all this for Peck, dear God—thank you so much."

Father McBride walked up and sat next to Peck.

"Hi Peck, good to see you."

"Hi Father, how you all are?"

"You looked intense in prayer, Peck. Need help with anything?"

"Father McBride—when you feel in your heart something's happening—like a sacrifice—but you can't prove it, what's a body supposed to do? Stop thinking or just quit? Even though he knows he's right? Any ideas, Father McBride?"

A sacrifice, Peck?"

"Yes, Father."

"Peck you attend Mass often."

"Yes, Father."

"Do you actually know what the Sacrifice of the Mass is, Peck? If you do, it may answer your question, my son."

"Tell me, Father."

"At the moment the priest takes a wafer of bread and breaks it up on a gold plate—"

"I see that, yes, Father."

"—and he says, 'This is my body.'"

"Yes, Father. I hear that too."

"Then he pours wine into a chalice and lifts it saying, 'This is my blood'."

"Peck, what do you suppose turns that wafer of bread and that cup of wine into the body and blood of Christ?"

"Angels, Father? I don't know. Who?"

"You do, Peck.'

"Me!?"

"Believers do, Peck."

"I do that?"

"Your faith does it, Peck. Your faith turns the bread and wine into the body and blood of the Lord."

"That's giving me chills, Father. Thank you so much."

"At the last supper, Peck—before Christ was crucified—he sat with the apostles, broke bread and passed around wine and said 'this is my body and this is my blood—do this in memory of me.' That's all a Mass is, Peck. It's a remembrance of the last supper—with our faith."

"Thank you, Father."

"Don't quit, Peck. On whatever you're working on, if you think there was sacrifice involved, believe it. You are gifted, my son. Have faith in your belief."

Father McBride stood and left. Peck prayed a bit more and drove home to the shotgun to see Gabe.

30.

PECK AND CHRISTIE walked into Larry's precinct and stopped at the front desk.

"Sergeant, can I have a pad and some markers?"

"You need the disc player today, friend?"

"Nah-nah, thanks."

Peck and Christie sat across from each other. The only difference this morning was the Grande chicory coffees and bag of powdered beignets Peck brought for the occasion. He raised his coffee in toast.

"Here's to you getting your confidence back, Christie. Those two babies will be blessed with a strong momma, dass for true."

"Thank you Peck. I really do appreciate you. Where do we start today?"

"You were telling me about being locked in a room somewhere and somebody slapped your face when you said you weren't hungry. Then you told me that some female voice was telling somebody to bring the Lord in or something like that."

"Yes."

"Just talk to me, cher. Tell me things you're thinking about. Things you remember."

"I remember the smell of bread, like a bakery."

"Ah *oui*."

"I remember counting when they put me in the truck again and began driving."

"Counting?"

"Counting—counting to myself."

"Where were they taking you?"

"I didn't know when they started, nobody said anything. They just drove. I just remember counting."

"What do you mean, counting? Counting sounds you heard, cher? Counting different voices? What were you counting, Christie?"

"I was counting seconds. I teach my preschoolers how to count seconds like on a clock—thousand one, thousand two—like that."

"What you're saying is when you say *thousand one* it's like saying it's a *second* on the clock, cher?"

"Yes."

"You remember how many seconds you counted?"

"From the time they started driving after putting me in the truck that time until they opened the door and made me get out before they drove away, I counted 2,501 seconds."

"I have to think on that one, cher. That might be important. Let me think on it."

"I remember hearing trains."

"While you were counting?"

"No."

"When you were locked up?"

"Yes, I don't know if it was day or night, but I could hear train sounds."

"Close by?"

"No, Peck, in the distance. I remember they sounded lonely."

"Ah *oui*."

"What else do you remember, Christie?"

"I remember hearing a cell phone or something ring."

"When?"

"They were pulling me out of the truck on Magazine Street."

"Did anyone answer it? Did you hear a voice?"

"I didn't hear anyone answering it, but just before the doors closed, I could hear a voice say, *'It's been burned … It's hot.'*"

"It's been burned … It's hot, cher?"

"That's what it sounded like. I couldn't tell if it was a man's or a woman's voice."

"It's been burned … It's hot," Peck repeated.

"Does it mean anything to you, Peck?"

Peck stood and walked to the easel with a pad of paper on it. He picked up a red marker. He wrote a one, a two and a three down the left side—leaving them all blank, waiting for his theories to be written in.

"One," Peck said. "My pickup exploded. It was a hot fire … it burned."

A tear rolled down from Christie's eye. She patted it with tissue, but nodding at the reality of the clue.

"Two," Peck said. "You smelled—how you say— bread like a bakery. Could be burned bread."

Christie nodded at the possibility.

"Three," Peck said. "I'm learning sentence structure in a writing class at Tulane, cher. I'm not so good at it, like the verbs and adverbs, things like that."

"You speak well, Peck."

"Ah, bébé, thank you for that. I'm getting better. But they's something with what you heard that is bothering me."

"There is?"

"Not bothering me. Maybe a better way to say it is, something you say has me curious."

"What did I say?"

"The voice said, *been,* cher—*it's been burned.*"

"I don't understand, Peck."

Maybe the voice isn't talking about my pickup burning, maybe."

"What are you thinking?"

"That's just it. Christie, are you okay with me taking you home to your babies and me going over to see my professor at Tulane? She'll know what it could mean—she's so smart."

"Do you think we're getting close, Peck? Was what I remembered helpful?"

"Oh, ah *oui*, cher. You did so good. Let me track some more and I'll call you, but if it's not until the next day, don't worry, okay? I'll call."

Peck tore the sheet from the pad and returned the easel and pad to the desk sergeant.

"Thank you, Sergeant. I'll be here tomorrow, okay?"

"See you then, son. Be safe out there."

Peck drove Christie to her shotgun on Magazine Street and waited for her to be inside. He then drove to Tulane's administration building and parked.

31.

"BOUDREAUX, IT'S NOT LIKE YOU to miss class but I haven't seen you for two weeks. Is everything all right at home?" Professor Berkin asked.

"Yes ma'am, everything is good at home, it's just that I've been working on some murder things with Lieutenant Gaines, is all."

"Have you been doing your reading?"

"Oh, I have been reading. I read *Old Man and the Sea*. I liked that story so much. It reminds me of my ol frien' Gabe and me and the way we are best frien's and work together. I have a John Grisham book too. No time to read right now. Sorry."

"To what do I owe this visit, Boudreaux?"

"I need some help trying to solve something, Professor Berkin. Somebody who was kidnapped couldn't see anything—they were blindfolded, but when the crooks let them out of a back end of a truck, she could hear somebody say, 'It's been burned … It's hot.' Can you help me think of what they were talking about, Professor?"

"It's been burned … it's hot. Interesting," Professor Berkin said.

"I can't think of anything, Professor. I come up with burned bread because the truck was a bakery truck we think—only because of the smells. Then I thought of the murdered guy who got burned. But wouldn't he be a 'he' and not an 'it' Professor?"

"Quite right, Boudreaux. Let me ask you—could the person they let out of the truck tell if the driver said, 'It's been burned … It's hot,' or was it a passenger?"

"Nah-nah, Professor. It was somebody who called. The voice came from a phone—somebody talking to the people in the truck."

"*Been* is a verb, Boudreaux. It sounds as if it's being used as news, almost like it was a warning?"

"These are bad people, Professor."

"Do you know if it was a bakery truck? The reference could be about a bakery order."

"I'm not sure."

"Do you know anything about the truck? Like how it sounds? Is it diesel? It could be it burns oil, Boudreaux."

"We think it was a van, Professor."

"Take my card, Boudreaux. Call me if you learn more. Email me anything you think might help me if finding out what '*burned*' is in this reference. I'll answer."

Peck thanked the professor went to the parking lot and called Larry.

"I was just about to call you, son," Larry said.

"Why?"

"Our man, Anthony, is ready for viewing—to be looked at."

For true, Larry?"

"No one will be able to tell what happened to him. He looks good, if a dead man can look good."

"Who did it?" Peck asked. "Who fixed him up?"

"Several people pitched in. Daughter of a friend of mine does facial rebuilding and makeup for funeral parlors—she volunteered to help."

"This is all so good, Larry, dass for true."

"He's at the morgue ready to be identified. I suggest you get her over to identify him, and we get him cremated and out of there. Time's an enemy when it comes to dead bodies and wax in this New Orleans heat, son."

"I understand. Let me talk to Christie and then I'll call Chris at the morgue. He won't say about how his face was, will he?"

"Chris won't say a word. Take her in—let him pull the drawer. That'll be it. A few days and you'll hand her an urn with his remains."

"Thanks for helping, Larry."

"And his widow will not get a bill."

"You're a good man, Larry. Thank everybody."

"Peck, when you get the time, I want to meet at the morgue to see what Chris found in the Rolex watch lady's autopsy."

"When I take Christie home, I'll call and go back and meet you there," Peck said.

"How's the tracking, son?"

"The more questions I get, Larry, the closer I know I'm getting to this thing."

"Where are you now?"

"I'm leaving a meeting at Tulane and going back to the precinct."

"Will we see you tonight, Peck?"

"I'll be there. See you on the roof at eight."

The call ended and Peck called Christie.

"Hi Peck."

"Christie, are you with the kids?"

"Bernadette's in school. Ally is with my best friend while I try to get job interviews."

"Cher, look nice, I'll be at your shotgun soon—I'm taking you to see Anthony. Lieutenant says we have to do that and then they'll have him cremated for you."

"I don't know."

"Now's when you need that confidence, Christie— just look Sunday nice, we'll—how you say—pay our respects ... and you can identify Anthony."

"Okay. I'm ready, I just have to put a dress on."

Peck picked Christie up and took her to the morgue. Chris pulled the drawer and uncovered the face of the body.

"Just nod, mum, if it's your husband," Chris said.

"That's Anthony," Christie said.

Christie wept as she reached and took the cover from Chris's hand and raised it higher.

"He has his bowtie on," she said.

"We had his bowtie, suit and shirt dry cleaned, Mrs. Bergeron," Chris said. "We wanted your Anthony to look nice."

"That was his favorite bowtie. I cut and sewed it."

"Would you like us to remove the bowtie as a keepsake, ma'am?"

"No. Thank you, but no. Let's send him to heaven looking nice."

"Yes ma'am."

Christie stepped toward Chris and gave him a cheek-to-cheek air kiss—it was as if she had read in the news that Anthony was badly burned.

"Thank you for making Anthony's face look nice."

"We may be a poor city, mum, but we're all family in spirit—when we meet our maker," Chris said.

"Mum? Where are you from?"

"Oh, I've been here all my life—my mom was full Irish from Dublin—just picked it up along the way."

"Thank you," Christie said. "Peck, can we go?"

Peck walked her to his pickup.

"Christie, can I take you to the precinct so we can talk a little more? We're getting so close. I can feel something breaking—don't ax me why—but I can feel it."

32.

PECK AND CHRISTIE WALKED into the precinct. Peck went up to the desk sergeant.

"Sergeant, we won't be here long—do you know if Maizie is upstairs?"

"I'll check, son. You want her to come down?"

"Yes, sir, thanks. She has my disc."

Peck and Christie sat across from each other at the table in Interrogation Room Three.

"Thank you for making me go see Anthony, Peck—for letting me say goodbye to him."

"Oh, cher, you don't ever have to say goodbye to that nice man. He'll be in your heart and he'll always be those babies' daddy, dass for true."

"You have such a pure way of looking at things, Peck. I admire that in you so much."

"When I couldn't swim, bébé—a bad man chained me under a porch while he'd go off to get bait shrimp to sell. Sometime it was all night he'd leave me. I'd pray for a full moon so I could pretend I could see my mammas and I'd tell her I'll be a good boy and can she come get me away from this bad man."

"That is so sad, Peck. You say you couldn't swim?"

"Oh, that's my way I say I was four—maybe three years old. That's how'd I say it before I learned to read and talk better."

"What a cruel man he must have been," Christie said.

"That's all we can say on that," Peck said. "My priest, Father McBride and my frien', Lieutenant Larry, say to never go back there in my brain."

"You're a good man, Peck. You're a blessed man."

"Thank you. Now can you tell me, Christie—can you think of anything else?"

Just as Christie was about to speak there was a knock on the door, and Maizie pushed it open and looked in.

"I can come back," Maizie said. "I didn't know—"

"Nah-nah, come on in, Maizie," Peck said.

Without disclosing why either was there, Peck introduced Christie to Maizie. Maizie handed Peck the disc.

"I found some more things—"

"You did?" Peck asked.

"I did—more things you should look at," Maizie said.

"Do you need me to step out?" Christie asked.

"Maizie, can you go ax the desk sergeant for the laptop thing and bring it here?"

Maizie left the room.

"Christie—" Peck started.

"Not to worry, Peck," Christie said. "I have calls I need to make. I'll sit out by the desk. Just let me know when you want me back."

"Thanks, cher. We're getting close."

"I pray for that every minute—so we can end with the questions," Christie said.

"Cher, before you go, how many seconds did you say you counted—when they drove you home?"

"Two thousand-five-hundred and one seconds."

Peck walked to a wall with a blank look on his face, stroking his chin.

As Christie stepped out of Interrogation Room Three, Maizie came in, carrying the laptop.

"You want to see the license plate on that truck?" Maizie asked. "I have part of it."

"Will you be here tomorrow, Maizie?"

"Yes—I'll be here from nine until eleven."

"Can we meet at nine, Maizie? I've got some things come up. I have to leave now."

"Clues?"

"Ideas is maybe a better word, dass for true."

"For sure."

"Okay, good."

"Peck, why would someone run in and out of a store like that—?"

"Not now, Maizie. Go with your aunt—tomorrow I'll look at the pictures of the license."

"Okay."

"Sorry I wasted your time today, Maizie. See you tomorrow."

"No worries."

Peck stepped into the hall, got Christie and they walked to his pickup.

"I have to take you home, cher."

"Were we finished?"

"Something important came up."

"About my Anthony?"

"Nah nah, cher. Father McBride gave me some advice I just remembered—and there's something in my brain and I need to stop thinking so much and let it—how you say—let faith help it settle, maybe."

"I think I can understand that, Peck."

"You're a smart woman, Christie."

"It's not about being smart, Peck. It's about being a mother."

33.

PECK DRESSED IN HIS BEST (and only) suit. He considered wearing a turtleneck, but he admired Gabe's look wearing a bow tie. He asked and Gabe obliged—not only to loaning Peck one of his bow ties, but tying it for him as well.

"My brother, how dashing you look," Gabe said.

"Thanks, Gabe. We do look good, don't we?"

"Two pieces of advice, son," Gabe said.

"Tell me, ol' man."

"You haven't seen some folks since your pickup blew up, son. Let them enjoy you—put it on pause tonight, son. Stop overthinking things."

"Thank you, frien'."

"My brother."

"What's the other thing, you say there were two things, Gabe. Two pieces of advice."

"Once a bowtie is set, don't be touching it, son. One wrong pull or tug on it and it'll come apart and an undone, hand-tied bowtie is impossible to tie again, after a couple drinks."

"Check," Peck said. "Good advice, ol' man."

"My brother."

Peck parked his pickup three blocks from Lily Cup's apartment building in the French Quarter. There was a private elevator to the roof, and Lily Cup and the lady who watered the plants were the only two with the keys. The building's rooftop would host many a full moon night with Lily Cup and Sasha sipping drinks, Sasha her martini and Lily Cup her rye. They would be dressed to the nines, and the evening would end by the two of them going to Charlie's Blue Note to dance jazz. If the wind stirred on the rooftop, Lily Cup would light a cigar—but the evening would be spent counting their blessings and praying no *gris-gris* befall either of them or their friends.

When the elevator door opened and Peck and Gabe stepped out, the four of them—Sasha, Lily Cup, Larry, and Charlie stood and applauded their entrance. Sasha was in a black Chanel dress.

As he stepped onto the roof, she ran to him and wrapped her arms around his neck. They didn't speak a word. They held each other—they knew what they both had been through together—cheating death—and what they always would be to each other.

Peck walked to the table holding Sasha up off her tiptoes, her arms wrapped around him like an octopus.

"Your face looks perfect, cher. No scars. Your dress is a wow, dass for true."

"*Merci.*"

"Is it new?"

"This is its first night out."

"How're the cuts on your leg?"

"Souvenirs, *mon cher*—souvenirs."

"Memories," Peck said.

Sasha smiled.

"The dress is my latest in Chanel."

"We must dance tonight at Charlie's, Sasha. I think we're related now," Peck said.

"What does the moon say, Lily Cup?" Peck asked.

Lily Cup raised her glass toward the moon in toast:

"We're all family here."

"And so incestual," Sasha quipped.

They raised their glasses.

"To our Peck—we celebrate that he's with us again and safe," Gabe said.

"We honor his dedication," Larry said.

"Let me down, Peck. You're wrinkling a Chanel," Sasha said.

They kissed as he set her down. He leaned and kissed Lily Cup and then Charlie on the cheek.

"Was there more to your pickup exploding than revenge, Peck?" Lily Cup asked.

"So much more," Peck said. "Working on it."

"Peck, whoever burned those surveillance pics was good—very good," Larry said.

"Hanh?" Peck asked.

"The ones you showed Chris and me—top notch."

"Did you say—*burned*, Larry?"

"I did, son. Good job."

"Larry, what does that word, *burned*, mean?"

"Pretty standard in forensics, son. When Forensics stops a video and zooms in on it for a highlight, they'll darken everything around what the camera is focusing on for a clearer picture. They call it dodging and burning—they're adjustments that help target or spotlight specific areas on a photo. That's called 'burning' it, son."

Peck set his beer down.

"I gotta' go," Peck said.

"What?" Charlie shouted. "You just got here."

"I've got to leave now," Peck said.

Peck kept motioning his index finger at Larry like the hammering of a woodpecker's beak—it was as if what Larry just taught him about *'burn'* had blown the murder case wide open.

"I have to go—it's important. Larry, can you give Gabe a ride to Charlie's Blue Note? I'll see you all there later, I promise. I got to go somewhere."

"Go!" Larry said.

Peck kissed Sasha and Lily Cup on the cheeks.

"You both look beautiful. I'll see you at Charlie's."

He ran to the elevator, jumped in and disappeared.

34.

PECK PULLED IN FRONT of Larry's precinct and parked. There was a night desk sergeant on duty.

"Desk Sergeant, earlier the daytime desk sergeant called upstairs for me and asked for a girl whose aunt works up there if she could help me with the—how you say—computer that shows the surveillance disc," Peck said. "I need to find her now."

"Sounds like you're talking about Maizie. She comes here, studies, and waits for her aunt to drive her home."

"That's her—Maizie—dass for true."

"Who are you? Why are you asking?"

"I'm Peck Finch. I need to talk to her, Sergeant. It's important to a murder case."

"Do you have a badge?" the desk sergeant asked.

"I'm private investigator Finch, Sergeant. I'm investigating for Lieutenant Gaines."

"You have any ID?"

"Can you find her, Sergeant?"

"I'll have to get orders from the lieutenant before—"

Peck pushed the contact button on his phone for Larry and handed his phone to the desk sergeant.

"Talk to me," Larry said.

"Lieutenant Gaines, this is Potter, night desk sergeant—"

"And Peck Finch is standing there?"

"Yes, sir. He is."

"Give the man anything he asks for, Sergeant. That's an order."

Larry ended the call.

"I'll have to call Maizie's aunt," the desk sergeant said. "I'll ask if she can have her call in. We'll have her call through the front desk phone for her safety and security."

"Good idea, Sergeant. Thank you. I'll sit over there and wait."

Fifteen minutes later the desk sergeant called Peck over and handed him a land line phone.

"Maizie?" Peck asked.

"What's up?" Maizie asked.

"Give me a second," Peck said.

"Okay."

Peck turned to the desk sergeant.

"Sergeant, can you step away for a minute?"

"Can't son. Have to man the desk at all times."

"What if I get Lieutenant Gaines to say it's okay?"

"Three minutes," the sergeant said.

He stepped away.

"Thank you, Sergeant."

Peck whispered.

"Do you live with your aunt, Maizie?"

"With my mom, why?"

"The desk sergeant called your aunt to get you on the phone."

"My aunt just called me. I don't think anybody there knows my mom."

"Maizie, how many of those pictures did you make of the traffic that drove by the jewelry store that day?"

"Lots. Maybe a dozen or more. Not sure, why?"

"Did you—how you say—burn any of them? The photos?"

"Seven of them, yes. Why?"

"You remember what they were?"

"Some were the arm reaching—some were of the van going by. One was the silver vase with roses in it."

"Has anyone else seen them?"

"My aunt for sure—maybe my mom. Why?"

"Just axing. Can you bring them tomorrow?"

"Yes—I have some really good ones."

"Would your aunt have seen them at your house or here at her office?"

"I used one of the computers near her office, so they would have been on my desk with me there. Maybe my mom, here—I don't know."

"Do people come see your aunt, Maizie?"

"A lot—for sure."

"So good, Maizie, dass for true."

"Is that why you wanted me to call?"

"Nah Nah—you told me you're good with math, right?"

"Yes."

"What if I give you clues and ax you to solve a mystery that uses numbers?"

"I can try. Whatcha' got?"

"Do you have a pencil, bébé?"

"I have my pen."

"Ready?"

"I'm ready."

"Somebody was in a—how you say—vehicle and they couldn't see—"

"Couldn't see what?"

"Pretend they were blindfolded, sitting in a car."

"Okay. I got it."

"From the time the vehicle started moving, this person who couldn't see started counting the seconds and never stopped counting the seconds until they stopped driving and let this person out."

"Okay, got it."

"This person counted seconds, like, thousand one, thousand two."

"I know what you mean, Peck."

"Before they let the blindfolded person out of the vehicle, this person had counted 2,501 seconds."

"Was that 2,501 seconds when the vehicle stopped or was it when the blindfolded person got out, Peck?"

"I don't know, Maizie—I didn't ax."

"That's okay. So, what do you need to know? What's the problem you want me to solve?"

"This person got out of the vehicle on Magazine Street, bébé—if I give you like the block number on Magazine Street, can you tell me where they drove from to get there?"

"Mom has a map I can use here, but I won't be able to bring it in."

"That's okay, bébé. We know that the vehicle driving away from that block on Magazine Street turned left."

"Left off Magazine Street. Got it. Do you know if any of the driving was on like Interstates or was it all in the city?"

"I don't know, bébé—but figure some Interstates, some city."

"Okay, I'll try to figure it out."

"See you in the morning, Maizie?"

"I'll be there at nine," Maizie said.

"Thank you, bébé."

"Maybe you better have a map there, Peck."

"I will. I know where I can get one."

"Good night, Peck."

"Night, Maizie."

Peck handed the phone to the desk sergeant, thanked him and left the building.

Walking up the alley to Charlie's Blue Note Peck was thinking of how it all began, right in front, on Frenchman Street. He looked for evidences of the explosion, but nothing was there but the nightmare's memories.

"Ice covers a lot of sins," he mumbled to himself.

He walked into a crowded Charlie's with sounds of jazz filling the air from the dulcet tones of a tenor sax played with a velvet touch. Peck waved at Charlie, mouthing a *'How you all are, frien'?'* Charlie pointed at him with a *'welcome back, bébé—you're looking so good in those fancy threads.'*

Peck stepped around Gabe and Sasha on the dance floor and found their table. His friend from the phone store, Aurelie, was sitting alone at another table. Without a word spoken, Peck offered his hand to her. She stood and he embraced her and turned onto the floor in a riff from a blues horn. The saxophone came alive again with mellow sounds of sadness and hope. Holding her close, Peck turned once, back, turned again. They accidently nudged into the dancing Gabe and Sasha. Gabe leaned over to tell Peck something.

"*You are my Lady*," Gabe said.

"Hanh?" Peck asked.

He turned Aurelie in closer to Gabe to hear.

"The sax," Gabe said. "He's playing *You Are My Lady*. It's from Freddie Jackson, a brother. That's playing for you two—welcome home, Peck."

"Who is that man?" Aurelie asked.

"He's my best frien' cher—ol Gabe."

Aurelie smiled. She reached her hand out and tapped on Sasha's shoulder.

"Ma'am, switch dance partners with me, please?" Aurelie asked.

Without losing a beat Sasha took Peck's hand as Aurelie took Gabe's hand and they exchanged partners while saying, "Honey, don't call me Ma'am."

The tracker in Peck let whatever was going down play out—what Aurelie was doing—he avoided jumping to conclusions. Gabe dipped Aurelie on a quiet riff of string bass solo and brought her up and into a turn.

Aurelie looked up at Gabe.

"I just wanted to meet the man Peck talks so much about. You're like a father to him. When you were in Carencro, I lived up bayou a few miles—isn't it a small world?"

"Peck told you about me?"

"I made my jambalaya and had two bottles of wine and tried to seduce him but all he did was talk about you and what a special friend you are to him."

Gabe grinned.

"Oh, he liked my jambalaya."

Gabe pursed his lips in a smile, leaned back as if he wanted her to see the happy surprise in his eyes.

"You make my heart sing, little angel," Gabe said. He turned her to the left, to the right and dipped her as the sax hit a low B flat.

As Gabe smiled into the possibilities of motion through another riff of horn and bass, Peck held Sasha close with gentle turns of their own, thigh on thigh leading and following, as if bound together.

Peck whispered:

"I read someplace, cher—that when a body saves the life of somebody else, the body they save has to spend their life—I don't remember how the rest goes."

Sasha kissed Peck on the ear.

"We saved each other's lives, Peck. Remember?"

"Ah *oui*."

"So, that must make us even, I guess."

"Your dress is perfect, Sasha."

"This old thing?"

"Oh, it looked new, cher."

"It is—just teasing."

Peck smelled her hair.

"My girls love it."

Always the admirer of cleavage, Peck tipped his head back for a peek and nodded approval.

"Who's the lady, Peck?"

"A frien', she helps me sometime. Just a frien'."

"I should have climbed your *William* on Mamma's houseboat that night we were in her feather bed."

"*Aye yi-yi*," Peck said.

"Sometimes I think about that night in Memphis," Sasha whispered. "You ever think about that night, Peck?"

Peck's response was a tight squeeze, his palm on the base of her back, pulling her into him.

"The night's still young, cher," Peck whispered.

Sasha howled.

They turned to the sounds of a bass solo, rocking back and forth with each strum.

"We have to find our Sasha a man, cher," Peck whispered into Sasha's ear.

"Sasha has all the men she can handle on the dance floor here at Charlie's Blue Note," Sasha said. "Her daylight alter ego, Michelle Lissette, could use a man."

"There's somebody out there for you, cher."

"Find me one who looks at me as a woman, an equal, and is not intimidated by an investment portfolio and we'll talk," Sasha said.

The dance ended and Peck and Sasha walked to the table. Sasha picked up a napkin and wiped lipstick off his ear.

A marine in his dress blues took Aurelie by the hand and asked her to dance. Peck watched as they left the table and turned into a riff from the string bass and drum.

"Gabe, can I eat beans and rice wearing an expensive bowtie?" Peck asked.

"Spots come out, my brother. This I know."

"No business tonight, son," Larry started. "But was it a good night with the 'burn' thing?"

"I think I'll have the answers in a few days," Peck said. "I'll know in the morning."

"How do you want to handle the store owner just coming back from his cruise, Peck?"

"Have you told him anything, Larry?"

"Like what?"

"Like the dead woman was his store manager?"

"He knows nothing from me, son. He saw the blood. He knows there was a body. Officer Downs would be discreet—tell him no more than necessary. I doubt he even told him the dead body was a woman. He only knows what his blind daughter might have told him. If he called the police they would refer it to me—he did and they did. I told him nothing. I even told him it'd be best if he'd not speak to anyone until after we met. He's coming in tomorrow."

"Can I have him alone, Larry? I need to ax him a few things. I feel good where my head's at now."

"He's all yours, son—with one caveat."

Peck typed "caveat" into his phone for a definition.

"Thanks, Larry."

"You spelled *caveat* right, Peck?" Larry asked.

"*Catch* would be a better word, Larry. When you're fishing for dinner—don't be wasting time with bait the fish have to think about. Use worms or shrimp—dass for true."

"The *catch* is—he's all yours—but I'll be in the room off in a corner."

"That'll be good—that caveat," Peck said

Lily Cup leaned in, grabbed Peck's lapel and pulled.

"That girl you danced with, do you like her?"

"I like her cher, but—"

"Now, smart ass—no more business—get your butt up off that chair, go get that girl—take her home, into your bed and get it on."

"For true?"

"She's been dancing with the marine over there and by looks of where his hand is, she's going to be toasting in his bed if you don't start taking care of business."

Peck watched Aurelie and the marine slow dance.

"She likes you, son," Larry said. "Go ahead. You need some relaxation. Take her home."

"I have to take a pee first, cher."

As Peck walked away, Gabe stepped over to the table with a fresh Chivas in hand.

"Where'd Peck run off to?" Gabe asked.

"Something's come up," Lily Cup said.

"Or it's about to," Sasha mused.

35.

PECK'S FIRST STOP NEXT MORNING was at Lily Cup's office. She was taking a bottle of rye out of a sack and putting it into her desk drawer. She saw Peck walking in.

"You and that lady take care of business?"

"She left with the marine. I think the marines landed last night. S'okay, though—I needed the sleep."

"I know what you must be going through breaking up with Millie, Peck. Live with the secrets—or get on with your lives."

"Why are you here so early cher?"

"Getting ready for a murder arraignment. Why are you here, Peck? I thought you had a meeting at Larry's precinct this morning?"

"I do. I just came to borrow some maps."

"Which ones? New Orleans or state maps?"

"New Orleans and one state map—can I use them? I'll bring them back."

Lily Cup took maps from a shelf and handed them to Peck. As he turned, she tweaked his butt cheek.

"How come I didn't get a dance with you last night?" Lily Cup asked with a pout.

Peck turned around. He set the maps on the desk, reached behind her and grabbed her butt cheeks and squeezed.

"Oh, cher, I can only—how you say—harass so many women at one time. We'll dance next time, I promise."

Lily Cup howled. "You're such a dick!"

When Peck walked into the precinct, Maizie was standing at the sergeant's desk, waiting.

"I have the room set up, Peck. There's a corkboard in there with pins. A paper pad on an easel and markers. We need a map, though."

"I have maps, bébé. Thanks for being here."

In the interrogation room, Peck opened his city and state maps on the table.

"Which one do you want, Maizie—you pick."

"The state."

She lifted it and held it against the cork board.

"Can we write on this?" Maizie asked.

"I don't think so."

"Can I pin it?"

"Are there pin holes in it now?" Peck asked.

"I see some, yes," Maizie said.

"Then we can pin it."

"Okay, good."

Maizie pointed to the far end of the table.

"I think you should sit over there," Maizie said.

Peck moved.

Maizie folded up the map that wasn't going to be used and then opened her folder and arranged things on the table.

"Ready?" she asked.

"I'm ready," Peck said.

"Your math problem was a time and distance problem. The fixed parameters were a number of seconds on a clock and miles driven and whether or not a correlation could be drawn between them. I had the fact that it was known that some of the seconds by the clock happened in the city and the variables were that some of them happened on Interstates or expressways. The first thing I determined— using a map—was the distance in miles from the block number on Magazine Street that you gave me to available Interstate entrances. I also had the vehicle turn left off Magazine Street as you told me. That left turn narrowed the possible Interstates or expressways the vehicle might have taken.

"Using estimates in traffic speeds—both heavy traffic and light traffic—in the city and traffic speeds on Interstates, which I got from the highway department's internet website, I've determined that the 2,501 seconds—or forty-one minutes—city and Interstate combined is twenty-nine miles. Using best-guess estimates—and this can only be theoretical, of course—I believe the distance of the drive the blindfolded person counted in seconds was twenty-nine miles."

"This is so good, dass for true."

With pins in her hand, Maizie turned to the map.

"Possible places where the drive may have started from are these. This pin—the city of Port Sulphur for one—this pin, the city of Raceland for one—Laplace is one—this last pin, Hammond Louisiana, is one. Picayune, Mississippi, is also within that driving criteria, but I'm not pinning that one."

"Why not?" Peck asked.

"The part of the plate I could see was not a Mississippi plate, Peck."

Peck gazed at the map as he would a foggy horizon of a swamp draped with Spanish moss. Each pin a cypress, each city its long roots with stories and mysteries of a deep swamp bottom crawling with live bait, crawfish, sea crabs and water snakes.

"Want to know what I found about that truck?"

"Tell me, bébé."

Maizie held up the pictures she printed out of the van driving by the jewelry store window.

"I was wondering, Peck, if the 2,501 seconds or twenty-nine-mile ride had anything to do with this picture I burned of the van driving by the jewelry store when that person ran out the door?"

Peck stood up, speechless. He walked to the door, thinking hard. He finally turned, went back to his chair and sat down.

"Maizie, I can't believe I didn't think it good like you did—that maybe these pictures of this van could be same as the—how you say—the math-problem vehicle."

"Oh?" Maizie asked. "I didn't—"

"Let's do this. Make believe the van you burned blowups of going by the jewelry store and the math problem/blindfolded ride are connected," Peck said. "This is like throwing out a trot line. We'll see if we catch something—maybe a clue or an idea. Let's pretend and say yes, they are connected."

"Oh, good," Maizie said.

"You happy with that? Why?" Peck asked.

"Because I had my homework done and I had nothing to do and I love solving puzzles and I began thinking and was wondering if they were connected—so I looked for websites that could help me find businesses by type in these cities I've pinned."

"What do you mean by type, bébé?"

"Types of businesses … maybe even types of businesses that would use vans."

"I don't understand computers, Maizie, but keep explaining, you do it good."

Maizie held up a "burned" close-up picture of the van.

"The sign on the side of this van was painted over. If you look at this enlargement, you can faintly see an *r* and a *y*."

"I see them, yes. *R* and *y*. I see them."

"I didn't have much luck looking through the white and yellow pages on the internet. It's too confusing, so I searched and found a Scrabble word-guesser and tried that."

"Scrabble?" Peck asked.

"Scrabble is a word game—you place letters down and the player with the highest scoring letters wins. The more difficult a letter is to find a word for, like a *q* or a *z*, the higher their value is in points."

Peck shrugged his shoulders as if she was speaking over his head.

Maizie wasn't deterred.

"So, I asked the Scrabble wizard to search and give me words that ended in *r* and *y*. Every word it could find. There were a lot of words ending in *r* and *y*. First thing I did was I went through the list of words and picked out businesses only that ended in *r y*."

Maizie wrote a word at a time on the board.

"Here are the words that are businesses and end with those letters: *bootery, cabinetry, brewery, bakery, cemetery, carpentry*."

"*Aye yi-yi*," Peck said.

"Is this helpful, Peck?"

"Maizie, you have no idea how helpful this is."

"So can I write a paper on it for school?"

"I have a better idea, bébé. How about you wait until we solve what we're trying to solve, and then you can ax us a lot of questions and write your paper then?"

"Like a first-person interview?"

"Like an interview, dass for true."

"That would be perfect. My teacher will love it."

"Such a good presentation, Maizie. Thank you."

"Can I go now?"

"Go, go. I'll pick things up."

"If you need anything else, let me know, okay?"

"I will—thank your aunt for letting you come."

Maizie stepped out of the interrogation room as Peck organized the space. The desk sergeant tapped on the door.

"Yes, Sergeant?"

"Your ten o'clock is here, Peck. Send him in?"

"That'd be good," Peck said. "Send the man in."

36

LARRY WALKED INTO Interrogation Room Three with a Mr. Melancon, the D & A store owner. Larry pointed to a seat at the table for the man. He then pulled a chair to a wall behind him and sat. Peck extended his hand.

"Thanks for coming Mr. Melancon. How you all are?" Peck asked.

"I've seen better times," Melancon answered. "Hurricanes and floods—oil spills."

"*Aye yi-yi*," Peck mused.

"Spare me the Hollywood pop culture *patois*, son. This is the Crescent City—not the *Big Easy* from the movies. If anything, our accents are more multilingual, like a Brooklynese—from the union dock workers' influences I suppose."

The sarcasm caused Peck to do a careful watch of the man's hand movements. It was as if he was studying his physical demeanor looking for signs, like he would watch the carapace of snappers making their way through reeds and into the swamp to determine if it was hunting or just moving into the sun.

"Hurricanes and floods—that's a metaphor, right?"

The man didn't laugh or respond. He had a look of fear and desperation in his eyes. Peck wanted to sympathize, but he was tracking. He was hunting and he knew he had to disarm the man and keep control of this pirogue.

"Mr. Melancon, my name is Boudreaux Clemont Finch. My friens' call me Peck—you can call me Peck. I grow'd up a gator bait slave for a bad gator man—My kin was buried alive when the dam busted and the Mississippi silt buried the whole town of Bayou Chene alive. I got my GED last November and I can read a book a week—and I'm reading Ernest Hemingway, but I truly like John

Steinbeck—so I'm sorry if you think my—how you say, *patois*—doesn't capture your respect. But it's real, sir, and I'm trying ever day to do better, dass for true."

Mr. Melancon didn't respond.

Larry spoke up as if to stir the pot.

"I bought a desk lamp in your store. Still have it."

"I don't know who's in charge, but whoever kept the horror of the killing in the store from my daughter, thank you. She's a delicate girl. She's on her way back to her mother now—but thanks to someone here, she only thinks she scared a burglar away with my gun. She doesn't know she hit a person."

"I have a theory why she didn't think she hit anyone with your gun, Mr. Melancon," Peck said.

"I'd be interested in hearing it, son."

"One of the bullets hit the stained-glass panel over your door," Peck said.

"That pane was old and rare," Mr. Melancon said.

"Not being safety glass," Larry said, "when the bullet hit it the glass shattered and it fell outside."

"Mr. Melancon, I'm thinking the sounds of traffic noises coming into the store through that window made your daughter think the burglar had opened the door and run away," Peck said. "I'm thinking that's when she dropped the gun and ran upstairs. She was scared and probably ran so fast she couldn't tell that what she may have thought was the door didn't close—because the traffic noise wouldn't have stopped coming through that window."

"God works in ways," Mr. Melancon said.

"Mr. Melancon, tell me about the store," Peck said.

"Tell you about the store?"

Mr. Melancon turned about to look at Larry.

"Lieutenant, I could be doing other things— bringing me down here—certainly we can do better than *tell me about the store?*"

"He knows what he's doing," Larry said.

"Mr. Melancon, did Lieutenant Gaines read you your rights?"

"I don't know why, but he did. He told me he wasn't arresting me, but because there was a dead body in my store, he was acting responsibly by reading me my rights if I was to be questioned."

"Okay—good idea."

"What do you want to know about my store?"

"Is the store your—how you say—your primary source of income?"

"It's my only source of income."

"I noticed on the sign it was open seven days a week and long hours. Are you in the store all those hours, Mr. Melancon?"

"Not all the time. No."

"When you're not there, who manages your store?"

"Whether I'm there or not, Marilyn Knotts is my manager. She manages it."

"How long have you known Marilyn Knotts?"

"Marilyn has managed the store for three years, I've known her for, I'd say, five years."

Peck watched Mr. Melancon's eyes as if he was watching a wafered morning moon. His instinct was that as with hunters in the swamps, eyes can tell a story. An unexperienced hunter would think the eyes of the hunter would be watching prey, but the experienced hunter would know the nose focuses on the prey—the eyes look for other hunters, cautiously darting about defensively to avoid becoming prey themselves. It's the same with liars.

"Marilyn would have come with me today, but she's on a cruise, and it doesn't come back for three days."

Hearing that—about Mr. Melancon thinking the deceased Marilyn Knotts was still alive—Larry bolted and stood up. Without letting Mr. Melancon see him, he signaled a thumbs-up to Peck to move forward with his interrogation and then a gesture with a thumb and little finger to his ear and chin, signaling to call him when he was finished.

Believing that animals can spot fear, Peck's face was stoic—a cold look he trained himself on by the age of eight, making his way through swamps. Larry left the room, closing the door quietly.

"Can you tell me about the cruise, Mr. Melancon— is your store manager, this Marilyn Knotts, on vacation? Did she win an ocean cruise like people do sometimes?"

"I was supposed to be with—" Mr. Melancon started. His face fell into his hands.

Peck waited, watching Mr. Melancon's body movement. It was as if he were wondering if Mr. Melancon really knew Marilyn Knotts was dead and was hiding it—or he truly missed her, as if he was in love with her.

Mr. Melancon was silent.

Following his tracking instincts, Peck took the lead.

"Mr. Melancon, let me guess. Just let me do the talking—for a while anyway. Can you do that?"

Mr. Melancon waited with a blank stare.

"I think I know what you're going through."

Mr. Melancon sat and waited.

"Mr. Melancon, you're afraid to talk—I have a feeling I know why—dass for true," Peck said.

Mr. Melancon didn't react.

"Mr. Melancon, you're thinking it's not over, I'll bet. This bad thing you went through."

Mr. Melancon stared at Peck with a look of surprise.

"Mr. Melancon somebody grabbed you three— maybe two days ago."

Mr. Melancon sat up straight.

"They taped your eyes and your wrists. A computer voice thing told you to not make noise or trouble or they would kill Marilyn, your store manager."

Mr. Melancon's shoulders slumped. Tears formed in his eyes.

"They locked you someplace and a voice told you there were cameras on you and if you took the tape off your eyes, they would kill Marilyn."

Mr. Melancon looked stunned.

"How do you know all this?"

"I picked the *Eight of Swords* card."

"Tarot told you all that?"

"Nah nah. My Tarot lady said Eight of Swords means feeling trapped, confined, backed into a corner, having hands tied."

"They taped my hands," Mr. Melancon said.

"They use fear, terror, and psychological issues."

Mr. Melancon stared down at the table.

"Mr. Melancon, you think Marilyn is really on a cruise?"

"She made the reservations. She called to tell me she would meet me on board. I don't know what happened after that."

"When they grabbed you, Mr. Melancon, did the van they drove you in smell like—bakery smells—like bread in the oven?"

Peck handed Mr. Melancon tissues.

"My name's David."

"Okay, David."

"How did you know this, Peck?"

"It's my job, frien'."

"I'm sorry for being rude."

"Nah nah, no worries, cher."

"It smelled like bread when they grabbed me. It didn't smell like that when they brought me back. When they brought me back whatever I was in smelled new. It had a new car smell."

"I know about what happened because it's happened before—to other people, David. Just the same way."

"You can't imagine how frightening it was. I had no earthly idea why somebody would just take me away like that—not tell me anything—and then bring me back and drop me blocks from my store blindfolded and drive away."

"It's what they call an MO."

"This really has happened to others?"

"Ah *oui*."

"But why? What satisfaction would there be in—?"

"They find two people who love each other so much and then without telling one why, they kidnap 'em and hide them somewhere, dass for true. They tell the other one about the kidnap and that they will kill the one they kidnapped if they don't do something bad—like steal something for them or do something like that."

"Animals!" David shouted.

"Ah *oui*. They get other people to commit the crimes and their hands are clean. That's the way Lieutenant Larry, who brought you in, would say it."

"Who were they going to use, Peck, with Marilyn on the cruise?"

Peck didn't answer.

"Thank God, my Patricia wasn't hurt—"

"Ah *oui*, David. Thank God."

"And thank God, Marilyn was on the cruise."

Peck didn't respond.

"I was going to propose to her on that cruise. She's probably worried sick I wasn't on the ship. I've tried to call her but her phone isn't working."

Peck lifted his phone and texted Larry to come back into the room. While waiting for him, Peck and David continued to talk.

"When they let me go, I was so afraid to talk to anyone, Peck. I just wasn't certain who I could trust—who I should tell."

"I understand, David. I kind of knew straight off that's what happened. I could see the hair pulled off your wrists from the tape they used."

David looked at his wrists.

"You have a good eye."

"That's what people tell me."

"Can you forgive me for being rude?"

Larry stepped into the interrogation room. He nodded to Peck for signals of whether or not David knew the MO and a signal asking if Mr. Melancon knew about the body's identity. With one finger up, Peck nodded his head yes as to the man knowing the MO. He put two fingers up for the second question—that the man didn't know about the dead person's identity. Larry pulled a chair to the table and sat next to David. He placed a palm on David's hand resting on the table.

"Mr. Melancon," Larry started.

"Call me David," David said.

"Marilyn Knotts is dead."

"No! No! No!"

"She was the body in your store."

"Don't say that!" David screamed.

"Marilyn Knotts was burglarizing your store."

Tears flowed down David's cheeks.

"That's a lie—Marilyn would never—"

David stood up, tipping his chair over backward.

"You're trying to trick me," David shouted.

"Nah nah, David—"

"These are all lies. You're trying to trap me—I'm going home."

Larry looked up from his seat.

"We know you were kidnapped, David. Why would we try to trap you?" Peck asked.

"Because you probably know about Marilyn's brother."

"We knew nothing about any of Marilyn's siblings. Why would her brother factor into this?" Larry asked.

"He's in trouble."

"We promise, David, neither of us knew anything about her brother. Didn't know she had a brother."

"She has two brothers. She needed money to get one of them out of trouble."

"What trouble was the brother in?"

"I'm not saying any more without an attorney."

"That's fine, David—you can go now," Larry said.

"Hanh?" Peck asked.

"I can?"

"You aren't under arrest. You aren't a suspect. Thanks for coming in. Sorry about your loss," Larry said.

"I gave Marilyn the money she needed to pay for his attorney and bail. She went to court for him and pleaded his innocence. She didn't have to steal anything. If she were alive, she would tell you the same thing. She called me after court and told me she was going home to pack and would see me on the cruise ship."

"What did they arrest her brother for?" Peck asked.

"Marijuana," David said. "He had two joints and because a cop saw him hand one of them to a friend, they arrested him for distribution. Can you imagine?"

"Marijuana is illegal, David."

"I know… but $25,000 bail for two joints?"

"Do you think the brother knows Marilyn is dead?" Peck asked. "The media hasn't announced it."

"I'm sure Marilyn's brother thinks we're both on a cruise. He's in Lafayette with an aunt, waiting for when he has to come back for trial. He's wearing an ankle monitor."

"David," Larry said. "These bastards kidnapped you and threatened Marilyn Knotts that if she ever wanted to see you again, she would have to steal two expensive Rolex watches and she had to make it look like a burglary."

"Marilyn's dead. How could you know what she was taking?"

"The Rolex watches were in her pockets—there were clues on the counter," Larry said. "The clues are pretty conclusive evidence."

"It's not making any sense. Marilyn has a set of every key. Why would she burglarize the store? I would have given her anything in it."

"They had her make it look like a burglary."

"But why?"

"So the police wouldn't suspect her and question her as a suspect."

"I don't understand—I would have given her the watches."

"But then you may have reported it to the police, David. They couldn't take that chance," Peck said.

"Whoever's behind this knows the system, David," Larry said. "They know how it works—its soft spots. They knew that if police ever interrogated Marilyn—a law-abiding citizen—she could be broken down in questioning and her answered testimony could possibly be traced back to them. They didn't want to leave any tracks."

"David, these are more than kidnappers. They're killers," Peck said. "Your Marilyn is one of the victims."

"They prey on couples devoted to each other. They play them like puppets—one not knowing why they're kidnapped or what the other is doing—one thinking if they don't do exactly what they're told to do, their partner will die," Larry said.

"Where is Marilyn?" David asked.

"At the morgue."

David clasped his hands and sobbed.

"We need you to identify the body," Larry said.

Peck stepped over to David and put his arms around him.

"I promise we'll catch them."

David was speechless, in tears.

"Can you tell me Marilyn's phone number?" Peck asked.

David wrote the number on a slip of paper and handed it to him. Peck texted it to Aurelie and messaged, *"Can you see if Lillian Meyer called this number?"*

"Did Marilyn know your daughter was upstairs?" Peck asked.

"No, she didn't—the cruise was spur of the moment. Marilyn didn't know I was going to propose. She didn't know had I asked my daughter to come and watch the parrot."

"Can I talk to you again if I need something, David?" Peck asked.

"You'll have to come to the store. I have to repair the damage and get it reopened somehow."

"Keeping yourself busy is the best thing, David."

"Broken glass everywhere. Bullet holes, blood—" he started, before breaking into sobs.

"David, one last question," Peck said.

David waited.

"When they locked you up somewhere, did you hear anything in the time you were there? Any sounds? Any voices?"

"I heard a train. I heard someone whistle like they were calling for a dog. I heard a motorcycle coming and then leaving. I remember because someone brought me food."

"What kind of food, David?"

"It was a long sandwich, like a hoagie. It had ham and sweet onions, I remember that. I can tell sweet onions by the taste."

"Ah *oui*," Peck said.

"I remember the motorcycle engine was turned off for a while. It started again and drove away."

"Thank you, David," Peck said.

"Lieutenant, may I go see Marilyn?" David asked.

"Are you in any condition to drive?" Larry asked.

"I can drive," David said.

"Follow me to the morgue," Larry said. "If you'll step out, give Peck and me a moment. I'll be with you in a second."

"I'll wait outside," David said.

"David, before you go, can I ax you something else just so I understand good?" Peck asked.

"Of course."

"You told me the vehicle—car, truck, whatever— they took you away in when they kidnapped you smelled like baked bread, yes?"

"It did, yes."

"And you say the vehicle they brought you back in didn't smell like a bakery, did I get that right?"

"Yes. It didn't have the same smell."

"One more question?"

"Okay."

"When they drove you back was it a long drive, could you tell—with your eyes being taped?"

"I remember thinking they were going to kill me and I remember saying a rosary to myself. I remember that. The ride was longer than I was praying but I did complete a rosary using my fingers, like I was counting beads on my leg. I remember after I finished the rosary, I made three Acts of Contrition. I was trying to do a final confession without a priest. I wasn't thinking about time."

"Thank you, David."

David left the room.

Larry stepped up close to Peck.

"Peck, are we through here?"

"Purdy much," Peck said. "With him anyway—for now."

"I liked your approach, Peck. You nailed it—kept him in the hunt, held his interest, didn't intimidate him. He answered what you needed to know."

"Larry, this is the same MO as the dead daddy on Magazine Street."

"Think you have a fix on things, do you, Peck?"

"I think purdy much, *oui*."

"Did you tell him about the ring in her stomach?"

"Nah nah, not yet."

"Talk to me."

"A trot line has many hooks, Larry. They're knot-tied to what're called snoods. I needed to leave some bait on one or two snood's hooks to just see if David slips and brings it up on this own—that he knows about the ring his Marilyn stole before we bring it up. He's probably innocent, but you never know what bait can do sometimes."

"You're still tracking, Peck—you're something."

"Until we have someone in our pirogue, Larry, everyone's a suspect."

"Call me if you get any closer, son."

"Larry, I'm purdy close, I'm thinking—but I have to go see some people. Can I maybe ax you and Chris to listen to what I got in the morning?"

"Your mind spinning is it, Peck? Need a hand?"

Peck pulled his tattered copy of Hemingway's *Old Man and the Sea* from his back pocket.

"Larry this old man in this book, he catches the biggest swordfish anyone has ever seen at that place he sails from, and now in the dark he's all alone with it bigger than his boat and he's got it tied alongside, trying to get it back to shore. He stares at the big old sailfish and keeps wondering if he's dreaming or is it real."

Peck finds the passage he marked with a sticky note.

"It's a great story, Peck."

"Listen to this part, Larry—

" *The old man looked at the fish constantly to make sure it was true. It was an hour before the first shark hit him. The shark was not an accident. He had come from deep down in the water…*

… Then he fell back into the sea and picked up the scent and started swimming on the course the skiff and the fish had taken. ' "

"That's when they came, right son? The sharks— they came up from below—devoured the ol' man's fish. I remember the book. Those scenes were chilling."

"Dass for true, Larry."

"Are you saying you can see the sharks, Peck?

"Ah *oui.*"

"So how can Chris and I help you?"

"You know chorizo, Larry?"

"I love chorizo, Peck—love it with light scrambled."

"Ah *oui*—perfect."

"So, what about it—you and your chorizo, son?"

"You know the skin on chorizo is tough, like rubber. If they don't peel it off, it gets—how you say— chewy. The skin."

"It's like chewing a knot in a balloon," Larry said.

"I'm chewing a knot in the balloon, Larry, so I'm wanting to tell you and Chris what I know and who I think is behind it. I can use your eyes to—how you say—listen to what I got and help point me, okay?"

"Text me where and when, son. We'll be there."

"I think I have it down to two chain links, but I got to see how they lock together."

"We'll be there for you, son."

"Oh, and Larry?"

"Yeah?"

"The ol' man in the book Larry, he had already killed some sharks with his knife and his oar, remember that?"

"I remember, Peck. He surely did."

"We're done with them sharks, Larry. They're dead."

"By 'done' you're saying, identified, right son?"

"Ah *oui*. They in the net. The case of the burned dead daddy, the case of the shot dead store manager—these cases, they are knifed."

"What's your point?"

"The sharks coming up from below are more of this kidnapping business going to happen if we don't put a stop to it now."

"Those new sharks are a metaphor, Peck?"

"I'll have to ax Professor Berkin—I don't know. All I know is we got to stop them with whatever we got so far."

"What's on your plate now, son."

"Going somewhere."

"Mind telling me where?"

"Somewhere to think," Peck said. "I have to think it good now."

Larry smiled and fist-bumped him.

They left Interrogation Room Three.

37.

SITTING IN HIS PICKUP, Peck called Aurelie, his contact at the phone store.

"Hi Peck, I have more information for you."

"Can you talk now?" Peck asked.

"I'm off today, but I ran in to work to check the number you texted me and I have an idea."

"Where you at, bébé?

"Want to meet at my apartment?"

"Ah bébé, I would, but I have a lot to get done today. I have to do a report in the morning."

"What do you have to report, Peck? Who's going to be there? Do you need my help in case they ask you things?"

"Maybe I will—but I don't want to get you in trouble going through people's phone records."

"No one has to know."

"I hear what you say but I don't want to do something that could make evidence—how you say— inadmissible. Lily Cup teaches me that word, bébé—it's a big one, dass for true. Private files might do that."

"Too late for that, Peck—but no one has to know where you got the information."

"How's that? How can I—?" Peck started.

"When I was a little girl, my Pépére would take me fishing, Peck. We'd sit in the rowboat watching the pretty ducks floating around the bayou. Pépére would patiently tell me stories while he baited my hook. It was like time stood still and I was the most important person in the world. I remember him telling me to hold what I knew in— not be a blabbermouth—but cut it up like bait, and if I use it in pieces people will always tell me what I may be thinking by biting the bait. They'll be honest and true, or they'll be scoundrels."

"Dass for true, bébé. I like that story."

"So, you don't tell them what you know or where you got it—you bait them and they'll tell you what you want to know."

"I like that, bébé. You're a smart one—you surely are."

"That way it comes from them, not from you."

"*Aye yi-yi*," Peck said.

"That number you gave me this morning, Peck?"

"Ah *oui*."

"Lillian Meyer called it six times."

"*Aye yi-yi*."

"The number she called never called Lillian Meyer."

"This is so good, Aurelie, thank you."

"Peck?"

"Ah *oui*?"

"Will we ever dance again?"

"Oh, for sure, bébé. Let me get through all this and we'll go to Charlie's Blue Note."

The call ended with a beeping into Peck's iPhone.

"Larry?" Peck asked.

"Peck, I hope you got what you needed from our David Melancon."

"Purdy much, I'll say. I wanted to know if the MO on the lady shot in the store was linked to the dead man, Anthony, and my pickup—and he purdy much proved to me it was."

"Good."

"Why you 'axing?"

"Our Mr. Melancon took one look at the body with the top of her head sawed off, shaved and stapled to the skull and he dropped to the floor with a massive heart attack."

"Is he dead, Larry?"

"It was a big one, but he wasn't dead when EMS took him away and to the hospital. He's alive, but I wouldn't count on him if you have more questions."

"These kidnappers are bad people, Larry. I think I'm ready."

"Talk to me, son."

"You told me to text you when I needed you and Chris?"

"I did."

"Can we meet at the precinct in the morning—nine o'clock?"

"We'll be there, Peck."

"Okay, good."

"You doing Charlie's Blue Note tonight, son?"

"Maybe tomorrow night, Larry. I have to go to Baton Rouge."

The call ended.

Peck called Aurelie again.

"Hi Peck."

"Cher, you said last time we talked that you had an idea. You never told me your idea."

"Ear buds, Peck."

"Hanh?"

"Bluetooth ear buds we can talk back and forth on. You can leave your iPhone in your pocket."

"I don't understand, bébé."

"You put earbuds in your ears. Before you go in to your meeting you call me and put the iPhone in your pocket—I don't go in tomorrow until noon. So, when you go into the meeting, I can hear what you're saying and if you need some information I have, I can tell it to you. I have copies of all the files here. No one will hear me but you—in your ear—and you won't know where I'm getting the information from."

"Why won't I know that, bébé?"

"Because I won't tell you. Ever."

"How do I get me some of those—"

"Ear buds?"

"Ah *oui*."

"I got some for you. You can pay me whenever."

"*Tu aime nourriture français, cher?*" Peck asked. ("You like French food, dear?")

"*Ce que tu pense, bébé—moi qui ai grandi à Church Point avec mes grands-parents—mon Momo et Pépére?* What you think, eh?" ("What you think, bébé—me growing up in Church Point with my grandparents—my Momo and Pépére?")

"You don't go to work until noon tomorrow?"

"Noon, tomorrow."

"You know that sexy dress you have? The one you wore that night we danced at Charlie's Blue Note?"

"Yes."

"Grab it, bring you some pretty shoes and I'm going to pick you up in front of your place, ten—maybe fifteen minutes, tops."

"We going dancing now, Peck?"

"To Baton Rouge, cher. You'll meet Elizabeth. We'll eat some good French food and you can teach me about that Bluetooth thing—okay with you?"

"Will I be back in time for—"

"My meeting is at nine, cher. I'll have you at your apartment by seven in the morning for sure."

"I'll be out front, Peck."

The call ended. Peck called Elizabeth and told her he was on his way for their special goodbye before she left for Paris. He didn't bother her with the details of his bringing Aurelie with him. Elizabeth knew his nature. Nothing Peck did would surprise her.

38.

THROUGH THE PEEPHOLE Elizabeth couldn't see Aurelie with Peck. She opened the door wearing nothing but a new chef's apron—folded down in front and tied at the waist, leaving little to the imagination—and a *toque* (chef hat), both from the new restaurant on the Left Bank in Paris where she would soon be moving.

"Oh, j'aime ton Elizabeth, Peck. Elle est comme tu l'as décrite," Aurelie whispered. ("Oh, I do love your Elizabeth, Peck. She's just as you described her.")

"I don't know who this girl is, Peck, but I love her already," Elizabeth said.

"Elizabeth, this is Aurelie, she's helping me—"

"Aurelie, do come in and make yourself comfortable while I say hello to my friend here," Elizabeth said as she wrapped her arms around Peck and kissed him passionately. There was a feeling in the room filled with taped up cardboard boxes like the moment had come—the moment they both were dreading—of being separated from each other's lives by a dispassionate ocean when Elizabeth moved to Paris.

Aurelie was sitting on an easy chair and Peck sat down on the sofa while Elizabeth took a bottle of chardonnay from the refrigerator. She uncorked it and brought the bottle and three glasses to the living room.

"I hope this will do—chardonnay?" she asked.

"It's perfect, for me," Aurelie said.

Elizabeth poured and then sat next to Peck on the sofa. She lifted her glass in a toast.

"À mon Boudreaux Clemont Finch, le détective privé—like Hercules Poirot." ("To my Boudreaux Clemont Finch, the private detective—like Hercules Poirot.")

"Too soon for that, cher," Peck said. But they all sipped none-the-less.

"You've solved the case, no?" Elizabeth asked.

"Nah-nah, not yet. That's why I brought Aurelie with me—hope you don't mind. I'm still working on it, but I have to use my brain and best I clear my head here with you and French food."

"And—with no offense intended—you brought Aurelie, why?"

Aurelie fended for Peck.

"Peck has an important meeting tomorrow where he's supposed to—how do they say it in the movies—wrap up the case for a lieutenant?" Aurelie said.

"Ah *oui*," Peck said.

"I had an idea for him and he didn't want to take the time to meet with me, so he said to come and we could talk while driving," Aurelie added.

"So, you work close with Peck?" Elizabeth asked.

"Let's say I do some research for him—maybe we should just leave it at that," Aurelie said.

"Aurelie is a good dancer, bébé. I took her to Charlie's one time," Peck said.

"I've never been to Charlie's, what is it—the Blue Note?—in all these years; we've never danced together, Peck," Elizabeth whispered.

"Cher, you have been my life since I was seventeen, the time we walked to your house in Breaux Bridge, remember?"

"Oh, I do—and I think of that day often, Peck. You were barefoot and you walked backward on the sidewalk in front of me, chattering away like a pollywog. It was hundred and three in the shade."

"Ah *oui*," Peck said.

"I hope I find love like you two have," Aurelie said.

Elizabeth's eyes glistened tears, as if she was thinking she knew she and Peck would soon be parting.

"Was it love at first sight?" Aurelie asked.

"For me it was the sparkle in his smile—his chatting away a mile a minute. Then it was the tub."

"The tub?" Aurelie asked.

"It was our treehouse. He was so innocent—my Huckleberry Finn. I scrubbed him up, clipped his toenails while he'd talk about a special knot he'd tie his snoods with and how he needed a sparkplug and did I know where he could buy one. Then I made crepes with jams and listened to his dreams of owning a crawfish farm, and he listened to mine of someday being a chef in Paris."

"Snood? What is a snood, Peck?"

"For fishhooks on my trotline," Peck said.

"I'll miss our 'tub' Peck. Our treehouse."

"Why don't you two go out and I'll just stay here and read or something?" Aurelie asked.

With that, Elizabeth jumped up.

"*Mais non, mon cherie*—by no means is tonight anything but a grand celebration. I must pull myself together. We will get dressed and go to the bistro and share stories and memories and we will sip and celebrate being a part of each other's lives. Aurelie, do you need something to wear?"

Aurelie lifted her baby doll dress from a sack.

"I brought this."

"Ooo la la," Elizabeth said. "Perfect."

It was a corner table at the bistro. In honor of Chef Elizabeth—soon to be "of Paris"—the table was draped with a French flag. There were two decanters reflecting a gentle candle glow in the center—a dry red and a chilled white—to limit server interruptions.

Elizabeth was wearing a golden metallic high-slit mini dress with slip-on sandals braided with pearls. Aurelie in her dazzling baby doll dress and thigh-high, sheer black stockings. Peck in black linen dress pants and a black silk top with onyx buttons—the outfit Elizabeth held in her closet for just such occasions.

They took their seats—and the night began with Elizabeth slipping out of her sandals, raising both legs, placing a foot on the chair between Peck's legs and one on Aurelie's thigh.

"On enlève nos chaussures et on s'admire de la tête aux pieds ce soir, non?" Elizabeth asked. ("We remove our shoes and admire each other head-to-toe this evening, no?")

Aurelie obliged Elizabeth's wish. She lifted Elizabeth's foot and kissed her big toe once before setting it gently back down on her thigh.

Elizabeth poured the wine and lifted her glass.

"Peck, you're looking confident," Elizabeth started.

"I am confident, cher, dass for true."

"But there's something in your eyes—something you're holding in."

"Nah-nah," Peck said. "It's about my work. How to tell you without—how you say—confusing the issue? I feel good about the clues we have and I think they'll help us."

"But…?" Elizabeth said. "I sense a *but* coming."

"But I need to—how you say—figure out the combination of clues I got so I can open the secret safe box and catch whoever it is, cher."

"You'll find the combination—in cooking we have common denominators—things that we learn will smell or taste a certain way when we mix them together. Make a list of ingredients in your cases, Peck," Elizabeth said. "Keep your nose open for that one ingredient that stands alone. It'll stand out."

"Aye yi-yi."

"That one ingredient could be your key. Look for secrets that may be hidden but appear in each of your cases. Sniff them out. Once you discover the one, answers will come easy."

"I'm worried more people are going to die and children will lose their daddies or mommas if we don't solve it soon."

"Make a list. Look into the keyhole, and you will solve the crimes," Elizabeth said.

"People are dying for no reason?" Aurelie asked.

"Let's not go into it more, bébé—let's not get too close to it here. Aurelie, your help will let me solve it, but let's don't add nightmares to our pillows tonight," Peck said.

"You have a beautiful soul, Peck. I'll miss you so," Elizabeth said.

"We'll always have the moon, cher. Don't forget that, my frien'," Peck said.

"If those murders are not solved, but close to being solved, Peck, why are you here in Baton Rouge? Might not the gravy burn?" Elizabeth asked.

"Cher, on this night Baton Rouge could be a million miles from everywhere. Distance is my strategy. I believe in the stars and in karma."

"Nobody on earth knows that better than me, Peck. I can't look at the stars, the moon and not think of you— not feel you in the room," Elizabeth said.

"I believe that the spirits of evil souls can hear the silence with me not being in N'Orleans and the guilty of them in N'Orleans will have a sense the chase has ended. They will get careless by overthinking their confidence— thinking that no one is tracking them anymore."

"Incredible," Elizabeth said.

"I learned this trick by standing in the lightning hole that was torn in the hollow of a cypress tree for three days, when I was nine or eight—trying to outwit that evil slaver, gator man by getting the bastard to believe I was gone or taken by a gator. It worked, and gator man gave up and smashed a whiskey bottle on a rock, got in his truck and

drove away, leaving a near starved eight-year-old—me—
free to escape and run away."

Aurelie lifted her glass of white in toast. "May I
make a speech?" she asked.

"But of course," Elizabeth said.

"Peck and Elizabeth, when I was a child in Church
Point with my grandparents—my Momo and Pépére—they
always tried to get me to be less impatient—they wanted
me to learn to listen more than talk, so I could learn more
things and grow up wiser."

"Smart grandparents," Elizabeth said. "Lucky girl."

"I remember them telling me an anonymous quote.
My Pépére wrote it down and I memorized it."

"Tell us," Elizabeth said.

Aurelie leaned in over the table and whispered.

"*Beware the quiet man. For while others speak, he
watches. And while others act, he plans. And when they
finally rest ... he strikes.*"

Elizabeth clasped praying hands to her lips, her
elbows on the table, her eyes closed, taking what Aurelie
said in with a deep reflection. She opened her eyes, pushed
her chair back, stood and stepped over to Aurelie, took her
cheeks in her hands leaned down and kissed her lips, never
taking her eyes off Aurelie's eyes.

"You have captured our Peck's soul. That was
perfect. *Merci, mon ami!*" Elizabeth said.

She kissed her again.

"Tonight, I plan," Peck said, sipping his wine.

Peck lifted his glass:

"To those in N'Orleans who will fall into my net—
they will bite into my snoods and soon be paying for their
crimes of creating fatherless orphans and lost lovers."

"Peck, you must come to Paris so we can make love
on the Right Bank and then on the Left Bank," Elizabeth
mused. "We must teach Paris what making love is—"

"In a tub, cher?" Peck asked.

"In the fountains, you sexy man. We will make love in every fountain."

Peck ordered duck a l'orange with the garlic-roasted asparagus. Elizabeth, the frog legs and mussels with the Achini di Pepe pasta. Aurelie, the raw oysters and a shrimp jambalaya. They spoke of dancing to jazz and of Peck's celebrated friendship with Lily Cup and Sasha and why Michelle Lissette in the business world turns into "Sasha" on her nights of lowcut cleavages and dance. How Lily Cup enjoyed the feel of a fine cigar, drank rye neat—especially before every murder trial. Elizabeth told of a cooking instructor she made love to in the vegetable room of the cooking school—and his wife on another occasion in the guestroom at a party.

"Je la laisse me séduire, je l'avoue. J'étais contente d'avoir obtenu mon diplôme. Elle était belle et le champagne m'a mis dans l'ambiance," Elizabeth said. ("I let her seduce me, I admit it. I was happy I had graduated. She was beautiful and the champagne put me in the mood.")

Aurelie admitted her shyness, and that playing strip poker with her friends across the hall may have been her wildest moments of adventure … as she once lost everything she was wearing at the time.

"May I ax you beautiful ladies for some help with my—how you say—dilemma, please?" Peck asked.

Elizabeth and Aurelie looked at each other and smiled.

"Does your dilemma happen to involve who you're sleeping with tonight, *mon ami*? I might save you from having to think about it," Elizabeth said, clicking her wine glass to his.

Peck smiled.

"Peck, when's the last time you made love to a woman?" Aurelie asked.

"Can you—how you say—define 'made love'?"

"Have you been intimate?"

"Cher, you and I kissed—Elizabeth and I kiss and play—and before Lieutenant Larry, I played with Lily Cup, but never the sex."

"Your kisses are intimate, Peck," Elizabeth said.

"I'll say," Aurelie mused.

Elizabeth smiled, raising a brow.

"Tonight, we are intimate, *mais oui*?" Elizabeth replied.

The three clicked glasses.

While Peck, Elizabeth, and Aurelie shared wine and stories at a bistro in Baton Rouge, Lieutenant Larry drove by the precinct and saw the lights on the second floor. The second floor was Forensics. Late night lights on the second floor usually meant murder. He pulled over, parked, and went up to see who was working so late. Through the glass in the door, he could see Mrs. Knapp at her computer. The light highlighted her quaff and eye makeup—she was obviously ready for a night out. She was dressed in a fashionable black cocktail dress. He tapped on the window so as not to frighten her. She turned, smiled, and flagged him in.

"Dressed to kill, yet a slave to your work," Larry said. "Our city is so much better served since you've joined our team, Mrs. Knapp."

"Why thank you, Lieutenant. It's Karen—Mrs. Knapp is my mother or my auntie."

"And I'm Larry. So good to finally meet you. Coroner O'Sullivan has high praises for you, Karen. I'm sorry for not having slowed down enough sooner to at least stop by and welcome you and introduce myself."

"I came on a whirlwind of bad *juju* in the city, it seems—crime is a part of life in Acadiana," Karen said. "I should have caught you in the halls and said hello. My bad."

"Where from?"

"I was in Atlanta, working on my doctorate. Your city made me an offer I couldn't refuse."

"Had to be more than money," Larry said.

"They were talking a new state-of-the-art forensics lab."

"If we can get the funding that we need, for certain."

"I think it was the baked Alaska served in the interview that did it."

"You'll find me at the city morgue more than downstairs," Larry said. "But good to finally meet."

"Thank you. My niece has helped someone downstairs with electronic equipment. Do you know a Peck Finch, Larry?"

"Peck is a private investigator, good man."

"My niece seems taken with how he thinks."

"Peck is one of the best—no question about it."

"He's made quite an impression on her."

"So, is there a late show, a midnight party?"

"Pardon me?"

"Something you're all decked out for, Karen? You're looking fine—must be something big going down tonight."

"Don't ever date an attorney, Larry—"

"Well, you got me there, Karen."

"How so?"

"Just so happens I am dating an attorney, and I'll have to plead the fifth. She's a criminal attorney—has a way about wanting to know everything."

"Mine too. That's just it, Larry. My man clams up. He'll keep secrets from me, claiming attorney-client privilege—but my life and work has to be an open book to him—like a daily journal. Sometimes I don't feel like I'm sitting at our dinner table, I feel like I'm sitting in the principal's office."

"Karen, my lady is so inquisitive—it's as if she would be happier if I'd FaceTime every investigation."

"My guy is so insecure; he thinks he has to buy me expensive things—that it's *things* that are what's important to me. Why don't some men get it? Most women don't want things. Women want—well, I'm not ever sure anymore."

"My wife is talking divorce. Her complaint was that I was never home. She didn't understand the equation that murder isn't nine to five."

"So, you're alone?" Karen asked.

"Separated and seeing my attorney friend who claims she's had an eye on me since my basketball glory back in Jim Crow days."

"She's white?"

"Lily Cup is a lawyer. She smokes cigars, favors eighty-proof rye, neat, and calls me her hot chocolate. And she reminded me one time that we're all the same hue when the lights are out."

"Oh my—she sounds like one of a kind."

"And as lily white as you."

"By your smile, looks like the *other departments* are good," Karen mused.

"A gentleman never—" Larry started.

"He tries, I'll give him that—but his always promising me he needs to shower me with 'things' gets annoying."

"He sounds insecure."

"Larry, if you become single again, will you marry your Lily Cup?"

"If Lily Cup wanted to, I wouldn't say no."

"Would you have kids?"

"Kids? I'd adopt. I'd make that clear up front."

"Adoption is good. Is it your only alternative?"

"Until America has this thing figured out, I don't feel a strong need to bring a child into the world. I've never said this out loud. Keep it to yourself, if you don't mind."

"Of course, don't even think about it. But you have such a respected career and following, Larry, doesn't that change—?"

"When *race* is removed from the dictionary—" Larry started.

They were silent for an awkward pause.

"Has your man stood you up, Karen?"

"His phone is off or out of range."

She looked at the time on her cell phone.

"I believe he has—by two hours now. No worries. I'll get caught up on some things."

Larry called Lily Cup's phone.

Lily Cup answered.

"Hey—you coming?"

"Lily Cup, we have a lady orphan here at the precinct—from Forensics. All dressed up and nowhere to go. Been stood up."

"Bring her, we'll get a bigger table," Lily Cup said.

They ended the call.

"Karen, booze is cheap, the jazz is hot, and they have the best red beans and rice in the city—how about joining us at Charlie's Blue Note?"

"Sounds like a plan," Karen said. "I'll follow you."

39.

BACK AT ELIZABETH'S APARTMENT, Aurelie was asleep on the sofa. Peck and Elizabeth were outside on the deck sharing a chaise lounge, watching the moon, listening to city sounds.

"Peck, I'm going to miss you. You think you'll ever come to Paris?"

"Dass for true, bébé," Peck whispered.

"Now doesn't that feel better?" Elizabeth asked.

"Cher, if this is going to be the last time I see you before you leave can you—how you say—grant me a wish?"

Elizabeth sat up, her face in his.

"Anything," she whispered.

"Can we do the tub?"

Elizabeth smiled.

"Our treehouse?"

"Ah *oui*."

"One last time?"

"Ah *oui*."

"*Je pensais que tu ne demanderais jamais.*" ("I thought you'd never ask.")

While Elizabeth was running the tub, sprinkling bubble bath powder in their magical "treehouse" in Baton Rouge, the band at Charlie's Blue Note in New Orleans was whining a riff of slow tenor sax and bass to a Joe Williams's *Every Day I Have the Blues*.

Gabe was dancing with Sasha, Larry was at the bar ordering drinks and Lily Cup had taken Karen by the hand, walked her onto the dance floor and began dancing.

"I'll lead," Lily Cup said.

Karen snuggled into Lily Cup's neck for a whisper.

"This takes me back," Karen said.

They turned and twisted with a mellow trombone riff blending into the slaps on the bass.

"Takes you back?" Lily Cup asked.

"Back to those high school dances with more girls than boys and we—" Karen started.

"A girl has to do what a girl has to do—like always—women having to make things happen for themselves," Lily Cup said. "I'd tape a flask of rye to my thigh. Tried to give the boys some incentive to ask me to dance."

"Ahh," Karen mused. "Hidden booze, your secret weapon. Clever. Naughty but clever."

"The secret weapon wasn't the booze, girlfriend. It was the hiding place."

Karen howled. "Didn't that invite unwanted touching and grabbing?"

"There was never any touching or grabbing. I'm a lady. Oh, their imaginations did plenty of imagining, that's certain. But if any of the boys took it beyond that, I'd deck 'em."

"You are something else."

"And the *rye* in my flask was tea. My dance card was always full because of boys' imaginations. Sasha taught me that."

"One of a kind."

"My daddy taught me ever since I was a little girl to listen to Leah Chase, the famous lady at the Dooky Chase restaurant. Leah always said, *'To be a woman you have to look like a girl, act like a lady, think like a man and work like a dog.'*"

Lily Cup turned Karen into a dip.

"Your Larry is a sweet guy," Karen said.

The song ended and Lily Cup and Karen walked back to the table where Larry was setting drinks down. They sat. Gabe and Sasha were soon to follow.

"Karen," Larry said. "I see you've met the inimitable Lily Cup. May I introduce you to a brother, Gabe, and this dancing lady, Sasha? Folks, meet a fellow cohort, a new addition at the precinct—Karen Knapp—forensics extraordinaire," Larry said.

Karen extended a hand. Gabe kissed it. Sasha took her seat.

"I love your dress, Sasha. It's phenomenal," Karen said.

"This ol' thing? My Givenchy?"

"I mean, it's absolutely—"

"Allow me to explain my garb, Karen. Here at Charlie's Blue Note, the few nights a week we come, I am Sasha. We come to dance—and to attract good dancers. I don my Givenchy or my Chanel. I let my girls out a tad and hopefully dance the night away."

"So it's more like a uniform," Karen said.

"Exactly—but then I met this big lug—Gabe—the best jazz dancer I've danced with ever—and that's a lot of dancing."

Karen laughed.

Sasha placed a hand over her cleavage.

"You think my strapless is too much?" she asked.

"Honey, you look devastating, Karen said.

"You wouldn't recognize Sasha in the daylight," Lily Cup said.

"Now that's hard to believe."

"In the daylight I'm Michelle Lissette," Sasha added. "I dress like a school librarian, boobs strapped in—showing seven-million-dollar homes in the Garden District to folks from all over the world who could write a check for them."

Everyone laughed and clicked glasses—just as Larry's phone beeped.

"Talk to me," Larry said into the phone.

"Lieutenant, Chris here—"

"Don't tell me, Chris—I'm about to dance to Louis Armstrong and you're looking at a body somewhere off in the night?"

"You sitting down, Lieutenant?"

"Where's here, Chris?"

"At the morgue."

"Uh-oh. I am—talk to me, friend."

"A twenty-seven-year-old woman with heavy amounts of blood caked in her hair and deep cuts on her arm that need stitches just walked into the morgue—"

Larry stood up, iPhone to his ear.

"I'm listening," he growled.

"—and she asked if her husband was here."

"Her husband—he works with you, does he?"

"That's just it—he doesn't."

"Do you know him?"

"I don't, Lieutenant. She was looking for his body. She's convinced he's dead. She thought she'd find it here."

"She thinks he's dead? Did she see something happen?"

"Lieutenant—that's your department. I don't question them. I just wonder where they all come from."

"Is she still there?"

"She is. I made her some coffee."

"Can you get her stitched up?"

"She'll have to sign some releases, but I can do something."

"I'll be right over."

Larry clicked off the phone.

"Something's come up."

"You only just got here, Larry," Lily Cup said.

"Sorry, I'm outta' here, folks. Karen, nice to meet you finally. Welcome to the best table, the best friends, the best jazz in town."

"Thank you," Karen said.

"My brother," Gabe said. "Karen is in good hands."

"Can I go with you?" Lily Cup asked.

"Not this time, hon."

"A hint?" Lily Cup asked.

"Stay here, dance. I'll call you later."

As Larry left Charlie's Blue Note, Karen's phone rang. She looked at the screen, stood up, stepped away from the table and answered it.

"Where have you been?" she asked.

"I'll be at the house in twenty minutes," a voice told her.

"Why are you breathing so hard?" Karen asked.

"Twenty minutes," the voice said.

"We need to talk," Karen said.

"Twenty minutes, goddammit!"

"Where are you?" Karen asked.

The caller hung up.

Karen clicked off and stepped over to the table.

"What do I owe?"

"You're our guest tonight," Gabe said.

"Are you leaving? So early?"

"Something's come up," Karen said.

Standing to bid her adieu, Gabe held out his hand.

"Is everything okay?" Lily Cup asked.

"Seems I'm a full-time fool for a partner who wants to be part-time," Karen said. "We're going to have 'that' talk tonight. Thank you all and I hope to see you again."

"Stay," Sasha said.

"Tempting, but I—"

"I say fuck the rude bastard," Lily Cup said.

Karen grinned.

"You're dressed to kill—he obviously promised you something more than a movie and pizza and left you high and dry," Lily Cup said. "Am I right?"

Karen nodded.

"I say let him stew," Sasha said. "Order a drink, stay awhile and dance."

Karen pondered—smirked a smile—and sat down. "You're right, fuck him," she replied.

The band started a riff of B. B. King blues with a saxophone side wail. Gabe stood and offered his hand to Karen. Karen looked at Sasha for approval.

"Be my guest, Karen, but I must warn you—" Sasha started.

"Gabe comes with a warning?" Karen mused. "Uh oh."

"Is that asshole a good dancer—the one you're going to have a talk with?"

"He's not bad, I'll give him that. Why?"

"Once you've danced with Gabe, hon …" Sasha laughed.

Gabe turned Karen onto the floor and paused, waiting for the saxophone whine to follow. Karen melted into Gabe's arms in his turns with her eyes closed as if she was dreaming of better times ahead. Lily Cup and Sasha watched.

"We've got to find her a real man," Lily Cup said.

Sasha looked at her watch.

"It's time for the midnight crowd," Sasha said. "Still a chance she could meet somebody tonight."

Lily Cup nudged Sasha, pointing to three men who came into Charlie's Blue Note wearing tuxedos.

"It could happen," Lily Cup said.

"Meantime, you're her dance partner, girlfriend," Sasha said.

"What am I—the lesbo dime-a-dance girl tonight?"

"Imagine she's Larry in a dress."

Lily Cup threw back her rye—gritting her teeth as she swallowed.

"You're such an—," Lily Cup started.

"Smoke a cigar," Sasha whispered.

40.

LARRY WALKED INTO THE MORGUE and Chris caught his eye and pointed to a side office where a woman was sitting with a cup of coffee. Larry gently rapped on the door and stepped in.

"Hi—I'm Lieutenant Gaines. And you are?"

"Carol. Carol Conklin."

"Is your head all right, Ms. Conklin? The blood—"

"It's fine."

"I understand you're looking for your husband?"

Carol opened her purse and handed Larry a photograph taken at their wedding.

"Lieutenant, have you seen this man?"

Larry examined the photograph.

"He's disappeared. I just know he's dead."

"You seem pretty certain. What leads you to think he's dead?"

"He'd never leave the house without leaving a note or a message on my iPhone."

"How many days has he been missing?"

"I'm not sure."

Larry knew it best not to banter or browbeat.

"I haven't seen this man, but we will make every effort to help you find him."

"It's so not like him. He would never not leave a message somehow."

"You say you don't know how long he's been missing?"

"I don't know."

Larry sat down.

"To help us find him let's start at the beginning. We'll do everything in our power to find your husband, but let's start with what happened to you. Tell me about the blood on your head—and I understand your arm needed stitches—"

"My leg too."

"Talk to me—"

"I escaped."

"Escaped from where?"

"It was like a small barn—an empty chicken coop. I cut my head on nails sticking out of the wall. It was dark— I couldn't see. I used the nails to get the tape off my wrists and then my hands were free and I escaped. I cut my arm and leg crawling through a small opening near the floor and I ran away."

"You say a chicken coop?"

"A chicken coop, yes."

"No wonder you're cut up. Chicken wire—nails, you say."

Larry stood and opened the door.

"Chris?"

"Yes, Lieutenant?"

"Can you get something to fight tetanus?"

"I have something. I'll bring it right in."

Larry sat down.

"Let's get you a tetanus shot so rusty nails and wires don't infect you."

"Thank you, Lieutenant."

"Where did this all take place? You ran from where? Do you know?"

"That's just it, Lieutenant, I don't know. I just started running, first it was through like a big pasture. I couldn't tell how big the pasture was, but it had a long driveway and it took a while to find a road. Then I was on Route 61 is all I remember—I saw the signs."

"How did you get there in the first place? The chicken coop. Did anyone tell you why you were there?"

"It all happened so fast, Lieutenant. Somebody grabbed me when I came out of our house to go to work and they blindfolded me—that's all I know."

"So, you were kidnapped?"

"Yes."

"Did anyone tell you why you were being kidnapped?"

"No."

"Are you athletic? Your escape sounds harrowing."

"I'm a physical trainer. I keep in shape."

"What you went through tonight took endurance," Larry said.

"I run a lot—not in competition for a while, though."

"Any idea how far you ran or how long you ran?"

"I won't lie. I stole a bicycle somewhere. I saw it leaning on a tree. As to how long and how far, my adrenaline wouldn't let me think of anything but not getting caught and of just wanting to get home."

"You have no idea who would want to do this to you?"

"Can I go home now?"

"Of course."

"I'm tired and I'm hungry."

"Where do you live?"

"Baudin Street, with my husband."

Chris rapped on the door, holding up a syringe.

"Let's get you vaccinated before you go. He'll have some papers for you to sign granting permission. I'll drive you home after. Can you give me a few minutes to make a call?"

"Yes—I'll wait."

As Larry stepped out of the room, Chris came in to administer the shot.

Larry touched Peck on his iPhone.

Peck reached for his jeans from the tub and took his iPhone from its pocket, saw it was Larry.

"How you are, frien'?"

"Need you here, Peck—meet me at the morgue?"

"I'm in Baton Rouge. Two, maybe three hours. What's up?"

"Kidnapping— victim escaped tonight, ran to the city and came to the morgue to see if her husband was here."

"*Aye yi-yi*," Peck said.

"Talk to me, son."

"Some things, Larry. Ax her what she does for a living. Ax her who she's met for the first time in the last few days. Ax her what her boyfriend or husband does. Ax her if anybody close to her has been in criminal court recently."

"That's it?" Larry asked.

"That'll be enough to get me started. Get that information from her. I'll leave now. We'll meet when I get there?"

"Let's do 9:00 a.m.—with Chris and me—at the precinct. I'll tell you her answers then."

The call ended.

While Larry was driving Ms. Conklin home, Peck was toweling off in Baton Rouge.

"Peck, should I ship my things before I leave for Paris—or have them shipped after I'm there and find a place?" Elizabeth asked.

"How long is your rent paid for, cher?'

"Three more months."

Elizabeth handed a dry towel to Peck and he began toweling her down.

"Go to Paris, cher, get settled—I'll come here and send the boxes to you when you want them."

There was a rap on the bathroom door. Elizabeth pulled it open to see Aurelie.

"Sorry, I need to pee," Aurelie said.

Elizabeth waved her in, pointed at the toilet and without waiting for them to step out Aurelie sat and did her business.

"Smells nice in here—I love bubble bath," Aurelie said.

"Bébé, I've got to get back. You okay if we leave now?" Peck asked.

"Something come up?" Aurelie asked.

"Dass for true. I need to be ready for the morning."

Aurelie finished her business, rinsed her hands in the sink, turned and hugged Elizabeth.

"You're going to light up Paris. Congratulations on your successes. Maybe I can go to Paris and see you."

"Tu es toujours la bienvenue, belle dame, tu resteras avec moi, bien sûr," Elizabeth said. ("You are always welcome, beautiful lady, you'll stay with me, of course.")

Peck was on the road forty minutes when his phone beeped. It was Larry. Aurelie was asleep in the passenger seat.

"How you are, Larry?"

"Peck, the kidnapped lady is a fitness instructor at a popular gym—has some private clients—seventy-five dollars an hour. A new client works at Tulane and Broad."

"Criminal court?"

"Yep—he's a lawyer."

"Anything else?"

"Yes. The kidnap victim—her old man is out of town."

"Where, Larry?"

"One guess."

"Too early, frien'—talk to me."

"You know the cruise ship our dead jewelry store burglar lady was supposed to be on?"

"*Aye yi-yi! Oui*—don't tell me."

"This kidnap victim's husband is on it, and it'll be back tomorrow."

"Something's not right, Larry."

"Such as?"

"If it's the same MO and she's been kidnapped—"

"Woman kidnapped? Husband gone missing? Sounds like the same MO to me, son. What's on your mind?"

"Larry, if it was the same MO, she wouldn't know about the cruise."

"She didn't know about the cruise—still doesn't know."

"Oh? So how do you know about the cruise?"

"I took her home—she went online and checked his emails and their bank account. Found nothing out of the ordinary. It was when I was leaving the house, I saw something on the ground behind the bushes. I picked it up. It was a copy of a delivery ticket."

"What's that, Larry—delivery ticket?"

"Some delivery person delivered something to the house. On it is, 'Time Sensitive Delivery—Passage to Key West'."

"She doesn't know how he paid for it—looking at the computer, bank accounts and like that?"

"He didn't pay for it. It's some smudged-out name. Might even be a receipt from a vending machine ticket dispenser."

"You believe she doesn't know anything?"

"Her story is convincing. I say she has no clue."

"When does the cruise get back?"

"Today at 4:00 p.m."

"What now, Larry? You call it, frien'."

"You think you've got enough for our morning thing, Peck?"

"Now I do—dass for true, Larry."

"See you at 9:00 a.m.—let's see what you got, son." The call ended.

Peck reached over and touched Aurelie on the arm, waking her.

"Where are we?"

"That's Lake Ponchartrain over there, bébé. We won't be long getting there … Aurelie, can I ax you something?"

"Sure."

"You think I can stay with you—my meeting is still on at nine and I need to keep—how you say—my head straight until the meeting."

"Hmm," Aurelie mused.

"What's that for, frien'?"

"Let me think."

"Are you playing poker, bébé? You fooling me?"

"What's it worth?"

"What you thinking, poker frien'?"

"You looked pretty cute in that bathroom."

"I was naked."

"I'm just funnin', Peck. Of course, you can stay." Aurelie grinned and stuck out her hand for a shake.

"Deal!" she said.

Peck grinned.

"Peck?"

"What?"

"Elizabeth was saying you needed to find a few ingredients that would open the magic safe. You think you have enough ingredients to figure out who's been murdering people?"

"I'll know if I do in the morning, cher."

Peck lifted his iPhone and touched Larry's contact.

"Talk to me," Larry answered.

"Larry, something important."

Larry didn't interrupt.

"Can you get Officer Downs to take chicken coop lady to where that cruise ship from Key West comes in?"

"What's on your mind, son?"

"Have them there early."

"Tell me why."

"Chicken coop lady can identify him—Officer Downs can detain him—"

"On what grounds?"

"If the MO is the same—we know he's been up to no good, Larry."

"Arrest him?"

"Nah nah—just detain him. Take him into a room and have chicken coop lady tell him we know she was kidnapped and we know he was blackmailed into doing something bad."

"Where are you going with this, Peck?"

"If this is the same MO, Larry—there's a good chance he stole things or did something bad on the cruise."

"Good thinking, son—what then?"

"Let him give what he stole back and let him go."

"I'll call you back."

Larry ended the call.

The New Orleans skyline came into view. Peck's phone rang. It was Larry again.

"Peck I called the police chief in Key West, Florida—woke him up."

"What for, Larry?"

"I asked him if there was anything going on in Key West that might draw a seedy crowd. He said there was a coin collectors' convention there. Lots of valuable coins."

"Larry, I don't see a guy off the street knowing anything about the—how you say—value of coins, do you?"

"I do if they're gold coins, son. A handful of gold coins are worth a pretty penny."

"Larry, we're in the pirogue—we come to a nest of baby alligators on the marsh weeds. You think it'd be smart to reach and grab one? That momma gator'll have an arm fast—chomp—I'll say."

"If the grab is at the convention trade room with all the security, true, Peck—you'd be right."

"Okay then," Peck said.

"But how about everyone on the cruise on their way to the convention—no one is protecting their rooms on the ship, son."

"*Aye yi-yi*!" Dass for true, Larry—good one."

"I have an idea. I'll call you back, son."

Larry clicked off.

They were driving through Metairie when Peck's phone rang again.

"This is Peck."

"I just spoke with the Coast Guard, Peck."

"What about?"

"How about I get the Coast Guard to stop the ship before it comes into port? Officer Downs boards the vessel with Ms. Conklin. Then takes her husband to the captain's cabin and do it there?"

"Good idea, Larry. If the ship isn't in port, the captain can return the stolen things because everyone is still on and no one's the wiser—"

"—or the loser, Peck."

"And then they let him go, right, Larry?"

"If it's only thievery—no one hurt. We'll do it all in such a way no one on the cruise will know who did it."

The call ended.

"Are you scared, Peck?" Aurelie asked.

"Ah *oui*—dass for true, bébé."

41.

PECK STEPPED FROM AURELIE'S apartment hours before his scheduled meeting with Larry and Chris. He seemed preoccupied and left without his usual morning ritual—a cup of chicory and two boiled eggs. He left Aurelie sleeping— quietly pulled the door closed and drove toward the precinct parking four blocks away. He started walking when Larry pulled over and lowered his passenger window.

"Jump in," Larry said.

Peck got in.

"Let me guess," Larry said.

"Go ahead," Peck said.

"You don't want anyone to see your pickup near the station—figuring if the precinct is infected with 'eyes and ears' they'd know its driver—you—would be in there."

"In the swamp, Larry—everything alive is two things—predator and prey."

Larry nodded. "Never thought of it like that, but you're right, Peck—the hunters and the hunted—all the same in the swamps."

"Precincts are swamps, Larry—think about it. They're two kinds—the good guys and the bad guys—"

"Pretty much," Larry said.

"There's always both in there. I don't want to make it easy for them—knowing I'm in there with a drive by. I want them to have to come inside and see if I'm in there."

Larry parked in the precinct's parking lot and paused before turning his engine off.

"Peck, are you thinking there might be a leak from here, inside the station?"

"Larry, do you remember the 'burned' thing you taught me about—what they do to surveillance video pictures?"

"I remember."

"That had to come from here. Whoever used that 'burned' word had to have access in this building or to someone who works here."

Peck and Larry walked up the front steps and went through the same door.

Peck smiled and said "good morning" to the desk sergeant and went to the interrogation room where Chris was setting up marker boards and corkboards.

"How you all are, Chris?" Peck asked.

"Moment of truth time," Chris said. "Can't wait to hear what your brain's come up with."

"Chris—can I ax you to move the boards from that wall to this wall over by the door?"

"You must have a reason. Will do," Chris said.

"Larry just reminded me of eyes and ears. I don't want anybody looking in the window reading charts— reading lips."

"Smart," Chris said. "And if my detective books are any help, by you not wanting anyone looking in—you suspect someone in the building could be a culprit or a leak or something."

Peck showed no emotion.

"Fish, snappers, frogs, crawfish, Chris— they all go to the same place—where the feeding is best," Peck said.

"So today this is the feeding spot, you think?" Chris asked.

Peck was stoic. He didn't answer. He helped move the boards. He set chairs so Larry and Chris could sit as an audience, watch him and listen. Larry stepped into the room.

"You're both here. It's after eight. Want me to start?" Peck asked.

"I'm all ears," Larry said.

"Go for it," Chris said.

Peck set a writing pad in front of both Larry and Chris. He lowered his head in reflection—blessed himself with a sign of the cross, looked up and began the only way he knew how—through simile and metaphor, like a schoolteacher. He did everything from memory.

"The Holy Trinity—bell pepper, 'onyon, and celery, is a base for most of what we eat, least here in Louisiana—can we say that?" Peck asked.

"Pretty much, Peck. Curious where you're going with this," Chris said.

"What's going to solve these murders and the bad things happening are the common denominators—the repeat things—the base we find the same in each one."

"Talk to us, son," Larry said.

"I'm going to give you words or things that happened or I heard more than once. They happened with burned man, the musician; they happened with the musician's wife, Christie, and they happened with Mr. Melancon, the shot-on-top-of-the-head lady's boyfriend."

"It's too early to know the Conklin story—the escaper," Larry said.

"It's not too early, Larry. The cruise ship is the same—the same ship from the shot-in-the-head lady and for Conklin. Tulane and Broad is the same as both victims had been in the criminal court. And Christie even interviewed for a job at the criminal court, so she was there too."

"I stand corrected," Larry said.

"Seems maybe Tulane and Broad is—how you say—a feeding ground."

Larry picked up his pen.

"Ready?" Peck asked.

He read slowly from memory the common denominators he had memorized.

"The smell of baked bread—the word *Lord*—the name Lillian Meyer—the criminal court—a motorcycle—

the saying of one Rosary and three Acts of Contrition—the counting of 2,501 seconds—or forty-one minutes—"

He paused, took a breath, and looked forward.

"Figuring time into distance, possible places—the city of Port Sulphur is one, the city of Raceland is one, and Laplace is one."

Peck leaned down on the table and almost in a whisper: "This precinct is one. Scrabble is one."

"You really thinking this precinct, son?" Larry asked. "An inside job?"

"Maybe not an inside job, Larry, but fed information from here. How would someone outside of this precinct know evidence we had was 'burned,' Larry? Remember that?"

"I remember telling you what *burned* meant and you leaving the party on Lily Cup's roof," Larry said. "But I didn't know you were having someone working on them here."

"The pictures I showed you were the burned pictures," Peck said.

"Burned here?" Larry asked. "Somebody here was helping you?"

Peck nodded.

"The leak had to come from here—and the girl who burned them didn't leak them. They had to be seen without her knowledge," Peck said.

How are you so sure, Peck?" Larry asked.

"She burned them at home. She brought them in a big envelope and would hand them to me when I'd come in."

"What girl, Peck. You say, 'the girl,'" Larry asked.

"Maizie—she's in high school. Her aunt works up in Forensics. She comes here after school and studies until her aunt can drive her home. Her momma works in Metairie and doesn't get home until six and doesn't want her to go home alone."

"This girl could be innocent, but a source for the other side without realizing it," Larry said.

"Nah nah, Larry. Find me who has access to this precinct and I'll find you the 'feeding spot,'" Peck said.

"You're getting a little too close to it, aren't you, tracker Peck?"

"How so?"

"Wouldn't that be 'find who had access to this precinct *and* Maizie's home,' Peck? You said she worked on the *burning* at home."

"Larry, work with me, frien'. There were two murders before there was any Maizie."

"That's all I had to know, son. Continue."

"You say feeding spot," Chris said. "That's a metaphor—right, Peck?"

Peck didn't answer.

"Answer him, Peck. If it's not Maizie working with you drawing the interest—making the precinct a feeding spot—what's the attraction, here?"

"I'm the attraction, Larry," Peck said.

"Whoa—now hold on son. You think just because you're doing some private investigation, you're the attraction?"

"Larry, it was my pickup that exploded, remember? I'm the attraction."

"It was exploded by traffickers, Peck—a bomb planted many months before all this started by traffickers who don't even exist now," Larry said.

"A bomb that exploded while a man was trying to steal it."

"What's the point son?"

"I was a witness, Larry. They know I was a witness to his breaking into my pickup and learned I did investigative work for you."

"I can't see how they'd make that connection after the explosion. How'd they figure you were more than just a victim, son?"

"Larry, how many *victims* get a police escort all the way from an alley off Frenchman Street through Metairie, where Officer Downs followed us the night it happened?"

Larry shook his head in amazement.

"I'll be damned," he said.

"By coming here, I caused this place to become the feeding ground," Peck said.

"Scrabble?" Chris asked. "Where's that fit?"

"Bootery, cabinetry, brewery, bakery, cemetery, carpentry," Peck said.

"It's Laplace," Larry said, looking at a map on his iPhone.

"Hanh?" Peck asked.

"Laplace is on Route 61, Peck. Last night's 'chicken coop' kidnap escapee ran and bicycled on Route 61 to get away."

Peck fist-pumped the air, celebrating closing in on a crime scene.

"Explain the Scrabble clue, Peck," Chris said.

Peck leaned down and lifted the receiver from the table telephone.

"Desk sergeant," a voice answered.

"Sergeant, do you know if Maizie is upstairs?"

"Not certain, Peck. You want her to come down?"

"Thanks, frien'—that would be good."

Peck hung up.

"I'll explain Scrabble when Maizie comes down," Peck said.

Chris nodded.

"It's a simple MO," Peck started.

"Walk us through it, son," Larry said.

"First step—they find two people who are inseparable—how you say—soulmates."

"I'll buy that," Larry said.

"Same," Chris said.

"It's pretty obvious they were finding the couples somehow at the courthouse—not sure how yet. But one being interviewed for a job there, her husband held over on marijuana charges and appearing there. One about to become engaged was there in court bailing out her brother."

"I'm liking where this is going, Lieutenant," Chris said.

"Number two, they figure a crime they want to happen. Could be they want a couple of Rolex watches— could be they wanted a ten-carat diamond ring—could be they wanted a pickup truck."

Larry and Chris nodded.

"Could be they want some gold coins," Larry said. "We'll know this afternoon when the cruise comes into port."

"Three, kidnap one of the couple and threaten the other that they do what they're told or the kidnapped one dies."

"Sounds pretty simple, Peck. How's it playing out with your tracking vibe? You getting signals on anything that doesn't make sense?"

"It's telling me the MO is complicated and that they could just as easily have demanded money for the kidnap."

"But they didn't, and why?" Chris asked.

Larry interrupted.

"That could be traced, Chris," Larry said. "Bleeps in bank account deposits, ATM photos of depositors—a number of ways. All tracks in the snow. This way—by having someone else do the crime independently, nothing could be traced back to them."

It was then Maizie tapped on the door. She was holding a tiny, fluffy golden Pomeranian puppy. She had her notebook and waited for invitation. Peck waved her in, reached, and scratched the dog's neck.

"How you all are, Maizie?"

"I'm fine," Maizie said.

"Nice dog, Chris said.

Maizie set her notebook down and held the puppy up for all to see.

"This is Byron," Maizie said.

Chris got up and scratched Byron behind the ear.

"Isn't he fun?" Maizie asked.

"Is Byron your puppy?" Peck asked.

"Oh, I wish. I'm dog sitting—my aunt is in a meeting, and they asked me to watch Byron."

"Is your aunt by any chance … the new lady up in Forensics?" Larry asked. "Karen?"

"That's her," Maizie said.

Peck interrupted.

"Lieutenant Gaines, Coroner O'Sullivan—meet Maizie. Maizie's been helping me—doing math and working the electronic gadgets. Maizie, these gentlemen are helping me try to solve crime."

"Hi," Maizie said.

"I have to ax you a question—can you see if you remember?"

"I'll try," Maizie said.

"So far I told some things that won't mean anything to you, Maizie—the smell of baked bread—the *Lord*—Lillian Meyer—criminal court—a motorcycle—"

"You're right. I don't know what any of that means," Maizie said.

"One Rosary —three Acts of Contrition—2,501 seconds—or forty-one minutes—" Peck said.

"I remember the 2,501 seconds one—that was the math problem you gave me," Maizie said. "I remember that one."

"Good. You remember doing the math and then after that the Scrabble idea you came up with?"

"Yes, but those were hypotheticals," Maizie said.

"I don't know what that means, but if I were to tell you we know the city was Laplace—would you know what Scrabble words you connected to Laplace?"

"I think I can figure it out. Let me look."

Maizie handed the puppy to Peck, opened her notebook and paged through, looking for a certain entry. When she found it, she looked at Peck anxiously.

"Go ahead," Peck said.

"Peck, am I allowed to tell secrets—like—you know, what I was looking for and how I figured it out?"

"Oh, sure, Maizie. You can tell them anything we were working on," Peck said.

"Okay, good. Well, I froze a video and burned some pictures of a van that was passing by the jewelry store supposedly when the robbery happened. The burned picture showed that the truck was painted over but we could see two letters through the paint—an *r* and a *y*. They were at the end of a word, so I searched my Scrabble app to find types of businesses that ended with *r y*."

"Young lady, you're amazing—please go into the field of forensics when it comes time for college."

Maizie grinned.

"So, here it is. *Laplace—cemetery* and *bakery*," Maizie said.

Just as she was making her report with her back to the door, a well-dressed man in suit and tie appeared in the window of the door. He was smiling inquisitively, seeking her attention and with raised brow, pointing at the dog in Peck's hand. Peck pointed to the dog, signaling an inquiry as if to ask if the puppy belonged to the man. The man nodded.

"Is that the man you're dog sitting for?" Peck asked.

Maizie turned and looked.

"That's him."

Peck held the puppy up, waved the man to come in.

"How you all are?" Peck asked.

"Maizie, I've been looking all over the building for Lord Byron. You gave me a fright, girl, leaving like that without telling me."

"I'm sorry," Maizie said.

"Byron here your puppy, sir?" Peck asked.

"My puppy—all $5000 of him and his papers—all mine."

"So, Byron here is Lord Byron?" Peck asked. "Did you call him Lord Byron?"

"He'll answer to Lord or Lord Byron."

"Well, I'll be."

When Peck had rattled out his common denominators, Larry made notes. With the word clue *Lord* mentioned by the visitor, he turned his notes face down on the table.

"Doesn't he look regal, though?" the man asked.

"Lord Byron certainly does look regal," Peck said. "This is an expensive dog, dass for true."

"There's a waiting list for them. He wasn't cheap."

"I can tell by looking at him. You must be important to be able to have a dog like Lord Byron. Where do you work—you mind me axin'?"

"I'm an attorney. Criminal court mostly."

"Ah, well, that would explain it."

"I do my fair share of pro-bono."

Peck turned away, catching Larry and Chris's eyes—raising and lowering his brow for them to see— signaling them to watch and follow his lead. He held the puppy up.

"This is *Lord* Byron, guys, can you imagine? Five thousand dollars for a puppy dog?" Peck asked.

Showing no emotion on their faces, they smiled as if interested in the cost of the puppy, but knew the hunter-tracker Peck better than most—and they had heard the word *Lord* in his preamble—so they had to know that Peck was about to start baiting his fishing snoods with deception and cunning in order to see if the owner of Lord Byron might start biting his hooks.

"Criminal court? Ah *oui*. That's sure enough means big fees."

"I get by. No time now, I've got to be somewhere. May I have my dog?"

Peck nuzzled the puppy with a kiss and held him to his chest.

"I know I've seen you somewhere. I hear you're very good, dass for true."

"Why, thank you."

The man reached for Lord Byron. Peck held the puppy close as if cuddling it—but held it.

"Imagine my girlfriend not wanting Lord Byron?"

"You, the criminal court, how come I'm thinking a name? You know a Lillian by any chance?" Peck prodded.

"Lillian Stallworth—my wife."

"Oh, wrong Lillian, I'll say. I was thinking Lillian Meyer," Peck said. "I know that Lillian—the Meyer one— from someplace."

"Maybe it was in school," the man said. "Where'd you go to school?"

"Nah nah," Peck said.

"It's the same Lillian," the man said. "Meyer was Lillian's maiden name."

"So, she got married—that's good."

"May I have the dog? I have to be—"

Peck scratched Lord Byron's ear.

"Didn't Lillian have a bakery?" Peck asked.

"Her brother. He has a bakery. That's probably what you're thinking of."

"Ah *oui*, that's it, I bet."

"They're partners in a hoagie shop—but he owns the bakery outright."

"Ah *oui*. So her brother is the Meyer, then."

"Yes, he's the Meyer—Meyer's Bakery."

"With the motorcycle," Peck said.

"George would rather ride a motorcycle than anything else—he's something," the man said. "Gentlemen, it's been nice but I have to be going. I have a—"

"Attorney Stallworth?"

"Call me John—but what's with all the questions? Don't you gentlemen have more important things to—"

"Can I ax you something, Attorney Stallworth, before you leave?"

"Ask, but may I have my dog? I'm in a hurry."

"You have a girlfriend and a wife?" Peck asked.

"Oops, did I let the cat out of the bag?"

"Seems so," Peck said.

"Oh well, it's a new day, friend—new age. No worries, we broke up this morning. Not that it's anybody's business."

Karen, in Forensics," Larry said.

"That's her—or rather, that was her."

Peck handed the dog to Chris.

"Attorney Stallworth," Peck said. "I ain't your frien'—dass for true."

Attorney Stallworth's face did a surprised double take that turned into a scowl.

"Just give me my dog," Stallworth said.

"Attorney Stallworth, I'm holding you on the suspicion of kidnapping—holding you on suspicion of felony murder."

"If this is some sort of practical joke, it's not the least bit funny."

He started toward Chris; his arms outstretched.

"Let's go, Lord Byron."

Chris turned away.

"Give me my fucking dog."

"There's a young lady here, Attorney Stallworth. Best we watch our language," Peck said.

Larry gestured for Maizie to leave. She stepped out, pulled the door and stood against the far hall wall, watching it unfold.

Peck continued.

"Suspicion of committing murder and suspicion of conspiracy to commit grand theft."

Stallworth shrugged and turned, reaching for the dog again.

"I admire your sand, you fucking illiterate coonass—but if you're not careful, you're about to become shredded and prosecuted. You're making up fairytales like you're on acid. Keep pushing me and you will pay dearly for it."

"You have the right to remain silent."

"You have no idea who I am, boy!"

"Anything you say can be used against you in court."

"You're messing with the wrong dude, you fucking ignorant peckerwood."

"You have a right to talk to a lawyer before we ask you any questions. You have the right to have a lawyer with you during questioning. If you cannot afford a lawyer, one will be appointed for you before any questioning, if you wish. If you decide to answer questions now without a lawyer present, you have the right to stop answering at any time."

"By what authority do you—?"

"This is a citizen's arrest."

"Fuck you."

He pushed Peck on the chest.

Peck grabbed his collar, turned him, and shoved him into the wall.

"Do you understand the rights I have just read to you?"

"Lieutenant, you're witness to this abuse. Don't just sit there," Stallworth growled to Larry. "I demand you arrest this man for assault and theft of my dog."

"Hands behind your back," Peck said.

Larry tossed Peck his handcuffs. Then he touched his shoulder mic.

"This is unit nine-eight-four—I need Officer Downs in Interrogation Room Three."

"Copy, Lieutenant," Downs responded.

"Fuck you all," Stallworth said.

Peck handcuffed him and reached in his pockets to retrieve the cellphone. He turned it off.

Officer Downs stepped into the room and grabbed the prisoner's arm firmly. Peck stepped back and purposely looked Stallworth straight in the eyes while speaking to Larry.

"Lieutenant Gaines, issue warrants for Lillian Stallworth and her brother, a George Meyer from Meyer's Bakery and let the State Police know they can find and arrest Lillian—and the bakery owner, George Meyer—in the vicinity of Laplace—"

"You ignorant bastard—you've got nothing. You will rue this day," Stallworth threatened.

"Officer Downs," Larry said. "Keep Mr. Stallworth here, in this room. I'll need an hour."

He stood and left the room."

"You have no right to detain me. I get a phone call—that's the law," Stallworth said.

"We'll be here an hour—lots of paperwork," Officer Downs said. "Mr. Stallworth, take a seat."

"Wait the hour, then book him," Peck said. "Without his ability to tip off his partners in crime an hour is all Lieutenant Gaines will need to make the arrests in Laplace."

Peck leaned over and looked Attorney Stallworth in the face.

"Do you understand the rights I've just read to you, Attorney Stallworth?" Peck asked.

"Fuck you, you've got nothing on me."

Peck leaned over the table.

"Attorney Stallworth, about how old is the chicken coop? I bet it's a real old antique little chicken barn, eh? I bet there's some good chicken stories out there in the field with wild animals, it could tell, hanh?" Peck chided.

Stallworth spit at Peck.

"Coroner O'Sullivan," Peck said. "I'll bet there's some purdy good DNA on the blood on them rusty nails in that chicken coop. What you say, Attorney Stallworth?"

Stallworth's head slumped.

Coroner O'Sullivan texted Larry:

"Lieutenant, have the State Police send their forensics team there too—check the chicken coop for human blood."

Peck stood up.

"Coroner O'Sullivan, ax Lieutenant Gaines to place a guard on that chicken coop so it doesn't accidently get burned."

Coroner O'Sullivan texted Larry.

"Protect the chicken coop from being burned— destroying DNA."

"Done," Chris said.

"Officer Downs," Peck said. "An hour in here and then, like Lieutenant Gaines said, book this slime crawfish snake on three counts of suspicion—kidnapping, two counts suspicion to commit murder, and suspicion to commit felony grand theft. Book him on all that, then let this murderer make his call. I'll send some coffee."

"How many counts for suspicion to commit felony grand theft, Peck?"

"We'll know when the cruise ship from Key West comes into port," Peck said.

Peck leaned across the table, sneering in Attorney Stallworth's face.

"Do you understand your rights?"

42.

LIEUTENANT GAINES'S PHONE RANG.

"Talk to me, Chris."

"Lieutenant—want to grab a coffee?" Chris asked.

"On my way to Laplace, Chris—what's up?"

"You believe how that unfolded, Lieutenant?"

"Watching it play out, Chris, I couldn't help but think how Peck survived the swamps when he was a boy."

"Had Stallworth eating out of his hand," Chris said.

"Chris, I believe Boudreaux Clemont Finch knows how to chum, and he made that interrogation room the feeding ground—and knew he was doing it."

"He did that today, you think, Lieutenant?"

"Chris, our man's been chumming for weeks—the precinct, probably Tulane and Broad, maybe even Charlie's Blue Note. Can you believe a bakery van and a chicken coop may have all the evidence and DNA we need to solve a lot of crime?"

"Sad, Lieutenant—our justice system criminalized."

"It's not the system—just some toxic reaper worms like Stallworth who worm their way in and use their law degrees to feed on the desperate. They paralyze innocents in criminal court for the first time."

"Lieutenant, what makes Peck so good? You think it's his tarot card reading?"

"I asked him, Chris. Know what he said?"

"Tell me."

"He said 'Tarot cards don't give answers, Larry—they give questions that need answers.'"

"What do I do with this puppy, Lieutenant?"

"Peck's checking pet stores and breeders to see if kidnapping was involved."

BOOKS BY JEROME MARK ANTIL

Genre: HISTORICAL FICTION
THE POMPEY HOLLOW BOOK CLUB
MYSTERIES OF POMPEY HOLLOW - 1949
BOOK OF CHARLIE – Spirit of the Pompey Hollow Book Club
(or) SUMMER OF SHADOWS, BODIES & BRIDGES - 1953
MARY CRANE – Séance with Sherlock
(or) SIDESHOW PICKPOCKET - 1953
HEMINGWAY, THREE ANGELS, and ME
(or) HEAVEN SENDS FOR HEMINGWAY - 1953
THE DELPHI FALLS TRILOGY - 1953

Genre: AUTOBIOGRAPHICAL
THE LONG STEM IS IN THE LOBBY - '58 to '61
From Bad Times to Good Times - How I found My Way
HOME ON THE RANGE – 1902 - 2021
RETURN TO TIFFANY'S

Genre: SUSPENSE/MYSTERY
ONE MORE LAST DANCE
THE HOODOO OF PECK FINCH
Sequel to One More Last Dance
MAMMA'S MOON - Duet Novel
(One More Last Dance & The Hoodoo of Peck Finch)
PECK FINCH and the HANGED MAN
PECK FINCH and THE EIGHT OF SWORDS

Genre: SELF HELP
HANDBOOK FOR WEEKEND DADS…and Anytime
grandparents.)

www.ingramcontent.com/pod-product-compliance
Lightning Source LLC
Chambersburg PA
CBHW030819210726
48290CB00002B/673